the Ravens

Katie f.

the Ravens

KATIE FAITH

The Ravens

Original illustrations by Damonza.com
Faith, Katie

ACKNOWLEDGMENTS

Completing this book has probably been the most exciting thing that has happened to me in my whole twelve years of living on this earth, and although I decided to write the words, it's because of all the support I've gotten that has given me the courage and persistence to finish it. I have so many thank-yous to give out that I'm not even sure I can fit them all on one or two pages, but I'm going to try.

First, to my writing mentor Shannon Mayer (who just happens to be a bestselling author... woohoo!) who allowed all this to happen and walked me through each step of the way. Thank you so much Shannon, I could never have done this without you.

Then to Tina Winograd, my first editor who was so kind to me and encouraged me even while giving criticism. You're so amazing, I can't even explain it.

I know for a fact if I forgot my mother and father and sister they'd be onto me for it. They have made it possible for me to do what I love and I am so grateful. You guys are always there for me. So Dad, even though you work lots of the time and don't really like reading all that much, I know you and Sister support me no matter what. And Mom, thanks for driving me to see Shannon and for all the time you have put into helping me finish my story. I love you guys. Thank you so much.

Becky and Katrina, for introducing me to Shannon in the first place.

My Montessori teachers, who taught me to write in the beginning. Thank you to my Kindergarten readiness teacher Christine Gross, my Kindergarten teacher Mrs. Sivil Sinclare, my Grade 1 to 3 teacher Mrs. Stephanie Custer, my Grade 4 teacher Mrs. Tiffany Campbell (I don't know if I would have written this without you), my Grade 5 teacher Mr. Shawn Burkholder who let me leave class early to write with Shannon, and my Grade 6/7 teacher Mrs. Anne Buchanan whose reaction I will be there to see when I hand her this book. Thank you all of you, you are truly wonderful.

To my Grandma and Papa, who always pro- vided ice cream and love in times of need. My whole family really - you all helped me at one time or another, even if you didn't know it. (I know I don't really talk to you guys much at family din- ners but I promise I'm listening!)

And to my Grade 6/7 friends who were in my class while I was writing. Jade, Jack, Natalie, Malcolm and Sylus who were just... well, hilarious to say the least. Thank you. (Feel free to yell at me if I spelt any of your names wrong)

Mwuahaha, I know I skipped you Olivia. And it was completely unintentio - intentional. Really though, c'mon now, I could never forget you. You don't honestly believe I could, do you, Olives? No, I couldn't. You're too important to be skipped. Thank you for being my friend.

And now for the person I've never actually met, but is just as important.

Robert Kiyosaki, my mom's favorite financial teacher who most likely changed my life, however indirectly. My Mom read his book "Why "A" Students Work for "C" Students and "B" Students Work for the Government" and it inspired her to help me pursue my interests, particularly in writing.

Thank you everyone. You've helped me such a tremendous amount. I can put a lot of things to words, but I can't put how thankful I am in them.

-Katie Faith

DEDICATION

To Shannon, you helped me so much for so little.

(And Mom, you can read it now)

PROLOGUE

THEN

Long, long ago, two types of people came to planet Earth. Though the original names are lost, they became known as the Ravens and the Slayers. Neither of these groups were human, in fact, this was generations before humans lived. Both types of people possessed different magical powers, and sometimes they were jealous of one another, but in the end they always seemed to work out their differences.

They were united, working together, never thinking one was different from the other. It was a golden age not only for them, but for Earth as well. The mostly blue planet grew and flourished until it became habitable for humans, at which time these peoples assimilated and lived side by side with the human race.

All was well for a time, until the two original groups became greedy for each other's power and started breaking apart.

Both the Ravens and Slayers were much stronger then than they are now; their powers were raw and new, their blood shared with the first most powerful who descended to Earth. When they broke apart with fewer friendships between the two, the greed grew and a grudge formed, each side wanting the others' powers, wanting to be the most powerful.

The next years were full of waging wars and terrifying bloodshed. Most of the populace from each group was decimated, leaving few alive. Their population, while previously almost double that of humans, was turned into hardly a speck in comparison. When they realized this, both factions agreed it would be best to go into hiding, as the humans could easily kill them at any time, in any place. So the leaders made an alliance with one another, not caring how much their people protested their decision.

This fragile alliance saw the two groups hidden together fewer than five months before someone accidentally killed a person from the other group with magic. The group whose member died demanded the killer be tortured, but they were refused. The two peoples battled again before both groups managed to flee, severing the alliance for centuries.

Decades upon decades later, a new crisis attacked those gifted with powers. A disease - a foul thing - went through the Ravens and Slayers. It seemed random with who it infected. Some lived miles away or fled and still caught it, where some could be exposed without catching even the common flu.

Half who caught it died, but survivors soon found they had lost their powers. They claimed it was like losing a part of them, and most went insane and killed themselves or fell into deep depression. Some survivors of the disease escaped these effects and carried on with their life through the difficulties, however these people were rare.

When one of the young survivors of the disease gave birth, the baby was unlike any ever seen from their race. It had different abilities, and after more of the children had kids, and those kids had young ones, they separated themselves, making a new race of people who called themselves Followers.

The Followers were immune to the disease that had created them; however, the surviving Ravens and Slayers still lived in mortal fear of this illness. When the leaders realized working together was the only hope of finding a cure, they merged. Most people didn't agree with the alliance, but they complied with their leaders' wishes, functioning almost together.

After finding the cure, the leaders hosted a feast in celebration, and everyone was happy until one woman fell ill after eating. Everyone pointed fingers, accusing each other of poisoning her. It ended in a bloody battle, and many escaped, but many did not.

That was the end of the third and final alliance the Ravens and Slayers ever had in their history.

CHAPTER ONE

MARRY

I stood on the steps of my new high school and took a deep breath. I did not want to go inside. Knowing my luck, today would only lead to more things I hated. Grade eleven would most likely suck, just like tenth grade.

Staring up at the building, it seemed to glow with an eerie darkness - and looking at it made me want to run in the opposite direction as fast as I could. I exhaled and walked toward the door anyway.

My parents had just divorced and my mom gave custody of Grant, my little sister, and me to Dad. He moved to Los Angeles, leaving my mother in Texas, where we'd lived my entire life.

Pushing my way through the crowd, I got to the main entrance. On the door was a list of student names and what class they were in first period. It was just for the new students. The old ones had to go to the office and ask for their list of classes for the day. I spotted my name.

MARRY CLAD – ROOM 306 – MS. PRATT – ENGLISH

Someone shoved me out of their path to get to the sign on the door, most likely giving me a bruise.

"What was that for?" I asked, glaring at her. She ignored me, though I was sure she heard. Her blond hair was in a ponytail and she wore jeans and a blue T-shirt. I felt anger flare in my stomach, then the students around us gasped. I looked back at the paper on the door. It was ripped in two. That wasn't much of a surprise - there were people pushing and shoving it constantly.

I let my anger at the girl go and walked into the school. The hall was packed with people, and dozens of lockers covered the walls, making it rare to see the light blue paint that coated them.

I followed along the walls, trying to stay away from the main flow of people down the middle of the hallway. In that moment, I missed my home and friends in Texas more than ever. Someone came up beside me - the girl who pushed me.

"Sorry, I didn't mean to push you earlier," she said. "I'm in your class, name's Lizzy, but you can call me Liz. Marry is your name, right - With two r's?" she asked.

"Yeah, I'm new here, from Texas," I said passing a door labeled Room 254 – Mr. Com – Math. "And, yeah, I get asked about the spelling of my name a lot. My mom wanted it to be unique while still using the name Mary, which is pretty common. She's weird about spelling." I was thankful I had pretty much mastered the art of erasing my accent, because I could tell already it would be embarrassing to have it in a place like this.

"Oh. I'm new as well, from Toronto," she told me as we approached a stairway leading to the next floor.

"You think our first class is upstairs?" Okay, so maybe this wasn't going to be so bad after all. It looked like I already made myself a friend, or at least someone who might help me navigate this place.

"Well, we won't ever find out if we don't look, come on," she said and started to jog, grabbing my hand and pulling me with her. "Bell's gonna go soon."

She was right; the bell was about to ring. I saw on the school website that teachers here took it very seriously when you weren't at class on time.

I jogged beside Liz as we went up the stairs,

finding our classroom and sitting at adjacent desks.

"Well, here we are," I said to Liz.

"Yep. What's your favorite subject? Mine is art ."

"Hmm, that's a hard one considering I'm bad at them all, but I'd have to say language arts. I personally call it laughing arts." I glanced around the room as the teacher walked through the door, gliding to her desk, placing a sign at the front of it that read Ms. Pratt.

I heard talking and looked toward the door, and the rest of the class came in, each chatting with, I assumed, their friends from last year.

I was reminded yet again of my group of friends in Texas, and longed to be with them. I had been pretending not to miss Texas when I was home with my sister, for her sake. But here it was painfully clear how lonely I really was.

The bell chimed and everyone hurried to be seated, but the chatter didn't stop. Ms. Pratt raised her hand, and everyone fell silent.

"Good morning, class," Ms. Pratt said, lowering her hand. "We'll go around and say your name. I see a few new faces and I'm eager to learn the names that go with them." She glanced at me, and a few others I thought were new, and then returned her gaze to the rest of the class. She pointed to the first person and said, "You start."

There was an odd silence for a second and then the person she pointed to began. "My name is Sarah Clarke," she said with a grin, flipping her shiny blond hair. Something seemed off about this Sarah girl. I couldn't put my finger on it, but she seemed... brighter than the others in the class. Then the next person spoke.

"My name is Toby Blake," he said, then looked around at all his classmates, his short brown hair shimmering in the light. I caught his eye for a second before he looked back at Ms. Pratt.

His blue eyes gave away the fact he was nervous.

"Also," Ms. Pratt added, "please say if you're new to this school, and if so where you are from. I don't recognize you, Toby. Are you new?" Toby looked nervous, but then shook it off.

"Yes, I am new here. I'm from Winnipeg, Manitoba." Several other students went and then it was Liz's turn, and after that, mine.

"My name is Lizzy Adler, but you can call me Liz. And yes, I am new. I came from Toronto."

And now it was my turn to tell the entire class my name and where I was from. I started to twiddle my thumbs and tap my feet on the floor, needing to fight the urge to get up and run out of the classroom. I didn't know why I was so embarrassed to just tell the class my name, but I was. I took a breath, hoping it wasn't unsteady. Everyone was watching me, waiting for me to say something

"My name is Marry Clad, from Texas." I couldn't stop my voice from being shaky, as much as I tried. Sarah Clarke giggled and whispered something to her friend. I glared at her, and then looked to the front again. Several books on Ms. Pratt's desk fell over, and she picked them up.

"So, now that we are introduced, we will get on with things. I'll pass around paper, but you can use your own if you want. You're going to write about your summer. If you're new, then you can write about your travel too," she said. "Any questions?" Nobody moved. "All right, begin, then."

I pulled out a piece of paper from my binder and wrote about how I, my Dad and my younger sister, Grant, moved here after my mom and dad divorced. How my mom gave custody of Grant and me to Dad, how we had to leave all our pets and animals in Texas, and I had to leave my horse and my donkey.

By the time I was done, English class was over, and I needed to go to Room 254, where I had math with Mr. Com. (Mister-Dot-Com, I'd decided to call him.)

Our breaks between classes were only five minutes and Liz wasn't in my math class, so I probably wouldn't see her until lunch. I grabbed my almost broken binder, hoping none of the loose papers would fall out.

"See ya, Liz," I yelled over my shoulder as I walked down the stairs. Lots of other kids rushed down to get to their next class, some of them bumping me. I heard someone clomping down the stairs, and turned slightly to see Sarah.

Her long legs carried her two steps at a time, and when she got in arm's reach of me, she shoved me forward, but not just a bump to get me to go faster, this was a push meant to make me fall over. I stumbled, and barely reached the bottom of the stairs on my feet. She pushed me again and I fell, all the loose papers in my binder falling out, making a mess on the floor.

Sarah and others stood laughing, following Sarah's lead. A small anger grew inside me. Why would she do this to me? I glared at her, resentment coming on strong. I gathered pages within reach, many shredded and torn. Holy cow, what happened to them?

Didn't matter right now. A crowd was gathering, about twenty kids, all giggling. Sarah waved at them, and said, "C'mon, I don't wanna be late because of this loser," then she was gone, followed by the others, and I sat alone.

I hated it. I hated all of it, the whole idea of moving here even. I never did anything to Sarah. Why would she embarrass me like that? I almost wanted to chase after her to ask, but that certainly wasn't an option. Maybe I would have wanted to punch her and hurt her if there hadn't been violence in my old school. People there used to punch and kick and hurt people who insulted them and... it was horrible. Someone once stabbed another kid and they got arrested. There was so much blood and chaos and... since that day I swore I'd never hurt anyone ever again if I could avoid it.

I backed up until I hit the wall, feeling tears coming on. I couldn't cry here, not where everyone could see me.

Scanning the walls, I spotted a door that didn't look like it led to a classroom and rushed to it. I swung inside, wiping my eyes as much as I could without messing up my makeup and trying to hold myself together. I missed Texas more than ever.

The door creaked open.

"Hey, uh... Marry is it? I saw you go in here. Are you all right?" a male voice asked, sticking his head in and looking around. I studied the inside of the door, staring at the red R on it. What an odd thing to put on a door. I took a deep breath, keeping my voice steady.

"Yeah, yeah, I'm good." He opened the door fully, letting light from the hallway shine into the room. "What's your name again?" I asked.

"Toby," he said. The guy from English class, then. Toby glanced over his shoulder at my scattered binder. "Is that your stuff over there?"

"Uh... yeah. Sarah - that girl from English class - pushed me and I dropped my binder. It's a little old," I said, holding my breath to stay calm.

"Wow. Here, I'll help you tidy it up. Let's try not to be any later for class than we have to be."

"Okay. Thanks. I appreciate it," I said, walking out to help him pick up the papers.
"Any time."

CHAPTER TWO

MARRY

"Yeah, that's it. Thanks," I said to the cafeteria clerk. I didn't really know who he was, but he was serving me food so I paid him some respect. Most of the tables were occupied, since I was kind of late to get my food considering I was at the end of the lunch line, but there were a couple empty ones near the back.

"Heeey," Liz said, coming up behind me, her food tray bumping into my side. I jumped, surprised. "Gee, I didn't realize you were so jittery," she said.

"I'm not jittery. Just didn't expect you," I said, turning to her and smiling.

"Whatever, bro. Let's find somewhere to sit."

"Bro?" I asked, following her to the back of the cafeteria, where there were less people.

"Figure of speech, my friend," she said. I smiled; she seemed to be in a good mood. I spotted a cleared table, and steered her to it. We sat, eating a few bites of pizza and fries. The table next to us was empty as well, and a few minutes later Sarah and her gang of friends sat there.

I overheard a particularly loud conversation from Sarah. I bet she was trying to make us hear.

"Hey look, Liz and Marry are teaming up over there - Those freaks." I glanced at Sarah and saw her and everyone at her table looking at us.

"Eww, can you smell that? I think it's coming from Liz. Gross," one of Sarah's friends said, holding her nose. The rest of their table did the same.

"Yep, definitely smell that," Sarah's friend murmured, though I assumed none of them smelled anything. I couldn't and I was sitting across from Liz. They were trying to upset us, and it was definitely working.

It was causing a small scene, and nearby tables hushed slightly, pretending to just be eating, but I could tell they were listening in to hear our reaction. Liz ducked a bit more, and picked at her food. I couldn't believe Sarah would go this far, in front of all these people. Surely a teacher should see this?

I felt bad for myself and Liz. Someone threw some sort of red fruit at Liz, and it splattered all over her shirt. I looked over, seeking who threw it, but couldn't pick out anyone obvious. Sarah's table laughed, and I saw Liz taking deep breaths to try to control herself. I couldn't let this keep going; Liz didn't do anything wrong. And she was in a good mood a second ago, too!

"Hey, Liz, you gonna just keep sitting there eating or what?" Sarah said.

"Nah, she won't do anything. She's too much of a coward," one of Sarah's friends said.

"And ugly," another chipped in. I had to do something about this, anything. Neither of us had done anything to them. I stood, glaring at their group. Everyone's drinks tipped over, spilling across the table, even Sarah's. She jumped out of her chair along with several others at the table and glared at me.

I ignored all their commotion. "You know what? Grow up," I yelled at Sarah as loud as I dared in the lunchroom, and left the cafeteria, Liz behind me. I stopped outside the door, leaning against the wall.

"Thanks," Liz said a little sheepishly. "She's been doing that to me all day. I didn't mean to drag you into it."

"You didn't. She's annoyed me like that too. And for the record, you don't stink and you're not ugly." I smiled, feeling good for standing up to Sarah; though I knew I shouldn't have since she probably wanted me to. She was looking for a reason to be mean and I'd just given her another one.

"Thanks. Got anything I can wipe this tomato off with?" she asked.

"I got a few tissues, here," I said, fishing in my pocket then passing them to her. She got most of the tomato off, but it would stain her shirt, which looked fairly expensive.

A couple of minutes later the bell for the end of lunch rang, and I rushed to my next class. Liz wasn't in this class either, and I wished for it to be the end of the day.

The stress of the day built up in me and the urge to find a sharp knife and cut myself hit me hard. I fought the desire . . . I'd put that behind me when we'd left Texas. I wasn't that girl anymore. But still it was hard for me not to think about it.

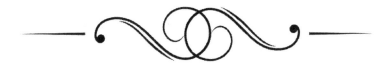

Finally, the day was over, and I was on the bus heading my way home. Toby sat next to me, going on and on about this new car he wanted. "It comes with these super awesome tires and the newest car engine in the *whole world*," he explained, though I don't really know the differ-ence between two engines. But I liked him, so I tried to listen.

"What type tires does it have again?" I asked, though I wasn't sure if I actually cared.

"Pit Bull Radial tires. They are the best for trails."

"Liar. We both know the best way to clear the trails is by horse," I stated "or more precisely, my horse." He laughed, I had been bragging about my horse, and it had become sort of a joke. The bus roared to a stop, I stood and made my way to the exit. My house was far from the school, and taking the bus, even though it went only part way, was faster than walking all the way. Toby came to my side. "This is my stop too," he said.

"Really?" I asked, raising my eyebrows.

"Yeah, do you want a walk home?"

I pursed my lips. "It's kind of a long way."

"I've got lots of time," he pressed. I decided not to protest. I nodded and continued on my

way. We didn't say anything during the trip until we got to my door.

Toby leaned over awkwardly and wiped his hand across the door. I stared at him.

"What are you doing?" I asked him. He leaned away, stepping back.

"Nothing at all, sorry," he said.

"Okay. See you."

"See you tomorrow."

When I got inside, everything was normal: my

sister played in the living room, and my Dad was on the computer in his office. My sister, Grant, just turned five, but because of the time of her birthday, Dad decided to hold her back from Kindergarten for another year.

"Marryyyy! You're home! I missed you soooooo much," Grant exclaimed, running up to me and hugging my legs.

"I missed you, too," I said, throwing my bags on the ground. "I need to feed the animals." She made an annoyed sound, then let me go.

"Why don't you stay and play with me?"

"They need food, too, you know," I said.

"You are always too busy to play with me." She sighed, then frowned and went back to playing with her weird and creepy Barbie dolls that looked more like they'd been attacked by serial killers because of their uneven-cut, knotted hair and missing legs. I flipped the channel on the TV to a kid-friendly show, then left the house and headed for the barn where my horses Tash and Sam waited for their dinner.

The grass around my house was a dark shade of yellow, crunching under my feet. The small bushes and plants were all mostly dead, not getting enough water, I assumed. Inside the barn, I gave Tash three flakes of hay and Sam a bucket of grain. I fed the rest of the animals hay, seeds, and grain then left the barn.

I walked toward a big oak tree that provided lots of shade, intending to sit and gather myself before going inside. The bark was a deep brown, and the leaves bright green. I shivered, and my skin crawled, though it wasn't cold. Larger bushes and plants were brown here, and all the grass was crunchy, making the place look very lifeless.

Then I saw something. I froze in my tracks. It was probably the most awful thing I had ever seen; the size, the look, the smell, everything about it was horrible. It was a rock, but the color changed it to something terrible, it was pitch-black, the darkest black I had ever seen. All around it, everything from weeds to small worms were deceased, not a single blade of grass remained alive.

I stared at it for a long moment; it was almost completely under the ground, with only the top of it sticking up. It wasn't really that bad in any way, just a black rock. Why did it seem so disturbing? I took a few steps back.

I hurried toward the house to prepare dinner. If I didn't, my dad would, and I knew his meals all too well: undercooked mac and cheese, or spaghetti without sauce. I decided on stir-fry for my Dad and I, with mac and cheese for my sister who didn't like anything that didn't come out of a box.

My Dad didn't even bother to come out of his office to thank me for dinner, just waited for me to bring it to him inside his office. I ate dinner at the table with Grant, in silence, only because Grant was watching TV when she ate; she hated talking when watching TV. While I ate, my mind wandered back to school. Oh, how I was dreading the next day.

After dinner, my Sister and Dad weren't feeling well, and by the next morning, it turned into something more like the plague. Somehow, I managed not to get it, and that in itself was a miracle. Dad had me drive them to the medi-clinic before school started.

The nurse entered the room, armed with a thermometer. "Someone isn't feeling well?" she asked. I waved my hand at Grant and Dad.

"Us two." Dad said, gesturing to Grant. The nurse approached Grant, kneeling down.

"Let me take your temperature sweetie - say 'ahhh.'" Grant did as told, opening her mouth. The nurse stuck the thermometer in, left it there for a moment then took it out. She checked the results, scowling.

"That is far higher than it should be. How old are you, sweetie?"

"I'm five..." Grant said weakly, her voice trailing off. The nurse's eyes looked about to fall out. She looked at Dad.

"You think you have the same thing your daughter has?"

"I think so... we have the same symptoms," Dad said, a little softer than usual.

"You should go to the hospital, right away. Her

temperature… it's too high." The nurse said, looking at Grant.

"Thanks for your help; I will take them to the hospital, right away," I said. She nodded, then left the room.

The hospital fiasco took all day. Fortunately for me, no school. I ended up getting home after dark. All alone. Flopping down on my bed, I let myself fall asleep and almost instantly had a nightmare. When I woke, my ears were ringing, and it almost hurt. The hair on my arms tingled; I wasn't the only person in the room. A cloaked figure stood by the window. I couldn't tell if he was looking outside or at me.

"Ah, finally, sleeping beauty awakens," he stated.

"Who are you?" I exclaimed, getting into a sitting position on my bed. If he said "I'm Batman" in a deep, breathy Christian Bale style I would've laughed, if I wasn't so scared.

"Hmm, ever thought I wondered the same about you?" he answered. I hated when people answered questions with a question.

"Why are you inside my room?" I asked, realizing he could very well be a murderer. Did I hear of one in this area in the news? This was LA after all.

"Because I want to talk to you," he said, not even the slightest concern in his voice.

"And you thought you had the right to invade

my house? But wait, coming in my house wasn't enough; you needed to burst in my bedroom too?" I crossed my arms, silently praying this guy wouldn't kill me.

"Well, yes, I did. And considering I could probably kill you if I needed to, I advise you to answer my questions and not be too bitchy about it."

Okay, this was scary. He just threatened to kill me. I didn't know what to do. Phone. I needed to get to the phone and call 911. If I could do that, I wouldn't even have to talk; they would hear our conversation and know something was wrong. I could get help. "Fine, my name is Marry Clad," I said, scared out of my skull. I shifted closer to the phone on the bedside table, and felt a tear start down my cheek.

"Ah, that's a girl. So, did you want your Dad and Sister to get sick? Did you ever wish for it?" he asked.

"No, of course not. Why would I want them to be sick?" I was offended by the question.

"You do know they are going to die without my help. The doctors can't do anything."

What did he mean about "without my help"; was he going to help me?

"You don't know that. The doctors might be able to do something. Besides, why would you help me? Who even are you? And what's up with the cape?" I asked, moving closer to the phone.

He seemed to fidget. "The doctors can't do

much, and also, the help wouldn't be free, you would have to give me something in return."

I realized I recognized that voice, but I didn't know from where. Who was it? Where had I heard this voice?

"Oh, yeah? And what's that?" I said. I didn't know why I was making this hard for him. He was clearly in control of this situation, at least a lot more than I was.

"You need to join the Ravens, and let me train you."

"What's that supposed to mean?"

"You join with me and let someone train you, and I will save your Sister and Dad."

"What do you mean 'join the Ravens'? Like a hockey team? If you knew me, Bat buddy, you'd know I'm not good with sports."

"You need to join my side," he clarified. Okay, this was getting weird, his side of what? I had a thousand questions, but had to hold them, and I guessed he wasn't giving me any more info.

"You think carefully about this. You have a while before we will make you choose, but keep thinking. I don't want to force you. Oh, also, I'd recommend against calling the cops, they will only make things messy for both of us."

I opened my mouth to say something, but before I could get the words out, I blinked and he was gone, leaving an open window behind him.

I knew I wouldn't get back to sleep, but I tried,

twisting and turning the rest of the night, scared
he'd come back and murder me.

CHAPTER THREE

MARRY

I survived the night. The next day, when I was eating breakfast before school, the hospital phoned. It wasn't good news. They said my Sister and Dad were worse, and they were puking a lot, even on medication that was supposed to stop the symptoms. Before the person on the telephone even hung up, I decided I was skipping school to visit my Sister and Dad in the hospital.

As I drove, I thought about the man who came into my house last night. Was it real? It certainly felt real. But maybe I was dreaming. Even so, what had he meant by join his team? A million questions ran through my head, and I almost hoped the man would come back so I could ask them.

I was outside my Sister's hospital room, my hand on the doorknob. Hopefully she was feeling better. I didn't like to see her like this. But she'd like it if I visited her.

I cracked the door open, going slowly so I didn't wake her if she was asleep. Hearing the hushed voices of nurses halted me, and I leaned in to listen to their conversation.

"Hopefully by tomorrow her hallucinations stop. I'm not sure what we can do if they don't," one of the nurses says.

"Maybe the doctors will prescribe a medicine that can stop it. The poor girl doesn't know what she's seeing."

"Maybe. When is the next..."

I opened the door wide, like I was already there and the nurses paused. I glanced at them, but went straight to my Sister's bed. She'd get better soon, I knew it. If I believed, it'd be true.

I kneeled next to my Sister's bed and held her hand. She moved her head to one side, and opened her eyes slightly, looking at me.

"How are you feeling?"

"Bad," she whispered so quietly I could barely hear her.

"You will be okay. I won't let anything happen to you, I promise."

She mumbled something I couldn't understand.

"I'm going to see the nurses and Dad, okay? Tell the nurses if you need something."

She made a small nod, then her eyes closed and she fell asleep. I headed toward the nurses, and before I got halfway, Grant started puking. The nurses ran to her, trying not to let it make a mess on Grant too much. Grant had an IV tube keeping her hydrated and she was on meds to keep her from vomiting too much, but from what I heard, nothing was helping. After Grant stopped, I talked to the nurses.

"How is she doing? Do you think she'll be okay?"

"Well, I do think she will be okay, but I also think she will have a rough couple of weeks fighting off this, uh, virus. We've been searching for anything this might be, and so far we haven't gotten any results, though the next lab results will be in soon. We don't really know what is wrong with her or how the virus spread at this point." We spoke in hushed voices, not wanting Grant to hear.

"Please call me if anything happens. If she gets worse or better, I want to know," I said.

"Okay, I will be glad let you know. I know this is a bit of a rough time for you, especially since you're new to this area."

"Thank you so much. Do you know where my Dad is?"

"Yes, he's just down the hall, room 296."

"Okay, thanks." I swept out of the room in three strides. I quietly opened the door and stepped inside. The room had deep red walls and silver trim. It was nice. The nurses saw me come in and greeted me then asked who I was.

"I'm his daughter."

"I'm sure he will be happy to see you, but don't be too loud." Her eyes told me she left off the words *he's not doing well*, for my sake.

"Okay," I replied, quietly sneaking to his side. When I greeted my Dad, he was pale and had an IV tube in him. I guessed it was the only thing keeping him hydrated, the same as Grant. The rhythmical beeping of the heart monitor assured me the patient was alive.

"How are you doing, Dad?"

"What's that on your face?" he mumbled.

"Where is it?"

"I don't really know. It's all fuzzy, like my eyes won't focus."

I touched my face. I couldn't feel anything. "I'll ask the nurse if she can see anything." I turned and looked at the nurse, and she smiled. "Is there anything on my face?" I asked. For a second, she looked surprised by my question, but then promptly replaced it with an expressionless mask.

"No, why do you ask?"

"My Dad said he saw something on my face."

She scowled. "He must be hallucinating."

"Did you think he would?"

"There is a possibility, and we thought it might happen."

"Oh, okay." I turned back to my Dad.

Over his heart, he clutched at his thin hospital gown. "It's still there," he said, and I started to get alarmed.

"It's all right. I don't mind," I said, smiling.

"Did you feed ... animals breakfast?" he mumbled.

"Good thing you reminded me. I don't think I did," I said. "I was eager to check on you and Grant."

"You better go feed..." His eyes drooped closed. The steady beat of the heart monitor stopped. An endless beep ensued. My father flat lined.

My own heart stopped in that moment. Time slowed as I whipped around to stare at the machine's straight green line flashing on the screen.

"DAD!" I yelled, grabbing his side. I shook him, pulling at his hands, willing him to wake up. The monitor continued to buzz.

"DAD! Get up!" The walls and floors shriveled up around me, and I was floating. I couldn't see. My mind spun. My body moved itself to the door and shoved it open - no way could my mind have figured that out. I distinctly heard myself scream for help, scream that he flat lined, scream all sorts of nonsense I couldn't comprehend, couldn't understand.

Because my father was dying. He was already dead.

I found myself shoved out of the way of the nurses and doctors and anyone else who showed up, but I couldn't see them. All I could see was the green flat line through my tears. I couldn't even see the walls of the room - I tried to focus but saw only emptiness. Like a long expanse of air with no sky, no mountains, no background.

There was nothing if Dad wasn't here.

More nurses pushed me to a corner, blocking my view, keeping me from seeing my father. I wiped my eyes, trying to wipe away those gathered around his bed, wipe away this moment and just see my father. But no matter, I still couldn't see. They buzzed around him, pushing on his chest, trying to shove life back into him.

There was a bump in the flat line.

And another, and another.

The doctor stopped.

The bumps continued.

Everyone seemed to wilt with relief, but I didn't stop crying. They let me pass, and I collapsed at my father's side. I took his wrist and felt a steady pulse.

I don't think I had ever felt more relieved in my whole life than I did in that moment.

Back at home, everything was quiet; no Sister

yelling, or Dad typing, just silence broken by the occasional whinny from a horse. I worried about my Sister and Dad. The house seemed empty without them, and I missed them more than anything. My heart ached for Grant's high-pitched voice, and for my Dad's music. He liked to play it when working.

I was sitting on the couch reading when the phone broke the silence. I looked at the caller ID: the hospital.

"Please let this be good news," I muttered as I promptly picked up the phone. After greetings, I asked about my family.

"They aren't doing well," she said. My heart tightened; had my father flat lined again?

"What's wrong?" I asked, panicked.

"Well, your Sister has started getting heart palpitations, and your Dad is having trouble breathing. However, I will assure you, your Dad has not flat lined again and he has a twenty-four/seven nurse with him."

Oh God, now I wasn't only worried about them being away too long, but it almost seemed possible for them not to ever come home. At least they had nurses. The hospital was the safest place for them to be right now, I reminded myself.

"Is that all? Any sign of them getting better?" I asked her, more hopeful than I probably should have been.

"No sign of them getting better, but give them time," she said. "Rest is the greatest cure. Also, maybe contact your Mother. She may need to stay with you." When nurses said *give them time* that was usually a bad thing, especially when the patient wasn't showing any sign of getting better.

"Okay, thanks for calling," I said, and hung up.

At that moment, all the grief, worries, sadness, and anger I had kept locked inside the past week, sprang up, and I was unable to push it down this time.

A part of me wanted to destroy. It was like a chunk of blackness coming up inside me, and a splotch of hatred and anger appearing out of nowhere. I heard things fall off shelves and whirled on them. There's no reason that those would fall. My head shook with all the emotion, and I didn't know what to do. The lights flickered uncontrollably and one burned out. I rolled off the couch, trying to get away from the chaos. Why was everything falling apart? Why was I here? The couch shook, and I closed my eyes.

I sat on the cold floor, pulling my legs to my chest as I let it all out. I cried over my Dad and Grant, how they weren't getting better. I cried over being in this awful place called LA. And I cried over the happy life I left behind and the loving family we once had. Finally I was done, able to push enough of my emotions inside.

However, the hatred and anger didn't leave. Those emotions wouldn't stay in. I wanted to be destructive, to ruin something, but I couldn't and I simply wouldn't. The world spun around me, and I thought back to last night, when the mysterious guy came. It was all so weird, replaying that conversation, barely anything that guy said made sense.

I was totally drained of energy. My head lay on the floor and the rest of me soon followed.

CHAPTER FOUR

MARRY

The next day, I was forced to go to school, despite my worries about my little Sister and Dad. In my classes everything was boring, nothing to do but listen to the teacher babble on and on about whatever he thought we needed to know.

Toby wasn't there, but I didn't blame him. I would have missed too if I knew this was coming. Of course, I couldn't survive listening to this forever, so instead, I drew on the back of my paper: a horse, Liz, Toby, trees, a sunset, anything that came to mind, not that drawing was much better than listening to the teacher.

"Marry?" someone asked as they touch my shoulder. I turn around, surprised to see a teacher behind me.

"Yeah?" I said.

"You need to come with me; we are going for a little walk," she said.

"Why?"

"It's about your Dad."

I nearly jumped out of my chair.

Sarah stood behind me. "I will come with you. It must be really hard, seeing your Dad and Sister hurt like they are." I open my mouth to protest her coming, or even touching me, but the teacher talked first.

"How nice of you to help your friend. Come on," she said. When Sarah caught up to us, she grabbed my hand in an almost reassuring way. In the hall, I expected the teacher to sit me down to tell me my Dad and Grant were dead.

But we kept walking; nobody saying a word. This was probably the counselor, taking me to her office, that's what I told myself. Halfway through the school, the teacher stopped, and turned to me. She stepped closer. I felt her breath on my face.

"Marry." Her voice carried a cold bitterness, like I was a criminal. "Just remember, I don't think you deserve what you will be offered today."

I barely saw her fist flying toward my head, and then nothing but blackness.

My eyes flickered open, and everything spun. I was in a room with a dozen others sitting across from me. My whole head throbbed, knives through my skull. I had to get away from the pain. I couldn't think anything else.

"Get her a healer."

"We can't do that. What if she refuses?"

"Doesn't matter - look at her. She's in pain and we can help her, so we should," the first voice snapped.

"Silence," demanded a third person, everyone fell silent. "Get her a healer; we don't have much time." I fell back into that deep haze, unwilling to come back to the real world.

I woke with such clarity and alertness, at first I thought everything that had happened to me was a dream. I felt wonderful, not just my body, but also my mind. Every part of me felt energized.

"Finally, sleeping beauty awakens," Sarah said. That was the same nickname the guy who invaded my bedroom used. The chair I sat in was no normal chair. Thick belts were attached to the arms, and they strapped around my wrists, keeping me unable to move. I looked around; eight people sat silently behind a long table, a roomful of people behind them.

"Why am I here and why am I tied to a chair?" I asked, trying to make my voice steady.

"The straps were for when you were asleep, but no point in taking them off. And you're here because we wanted you to be," Sarah said.

My eyes drifted from one person to another, and in the back of the crowd, I saw the mysterious cloaked figure who'd come to my house. He sat where nobody up front could see him except me, and even I didn't have a clear view.

"Why did you need to knock me out in the process of bringing me here? I would have walked in willingly." I wasn't sure it was exactly accurate, though.

"Look, your Sister and Dad are going to die without our help. There's nothing the doctors can do," Sarah stated.

"That's not true; the doctors still might be able to help them." My words were more to convince myself than Sarah. I had a feeling she was right.

"You're in denial. It's obvious they won't make it."

"They might be able to. They are strong."

"We could save them," she said. Suddenly what

she was saying sunk in. If she could heal them with an herb or something, I would do whatever they wanted for almost any price, if they could save them.

"You could?" I asked, hope filling my heart. I didn't question how, but I should have. Although I hated to admit it, they were right. My Sister and Dad's chances of making it through their illness was looking slim, if the doctors and nurses were to be believed.

This could be my family's only hope.

"Long story, but we'll only help them if you do something for us in return," Sarah said.

"What?"

"Do what Raven Master told you, join the Ravens."

Raven Master? Was he the guy at my house? My eyes rest on the cloaked figure near the back. I didn't want to say, "Yeah, sure," because I didn't know anything about it. The group could be a horrible gang that wouldn't let you leave after you'd joined. They could be murderers. But I might not get another chance to help my family. I decided to stall for time.

"Why does everyone want me to join the Ravens?"

"Because you're *valuable*," Sarah spat.

Valuable? What was she talking about? Sweat built in my armpits from stress, and I felt like running. Far away from everything. To a world less cruel and unfair, if only one existed.

"How am I valuable?" I asked, staring at her. She glared back.

"Again, it's a long story. You'll learn in training, *if* you join us." Sarah sounded bored.

"Where am I?" I asked, again stalling.

"You're in the Raven compound, and this is the council." She motioned toward the others sitting in chairs opposite me. "Join the Ravens, and we will save your Sister and Dad; refuse, and they will die." She seemed so certain.

The terrifying idea of my Sister dying at such a young age froze my breathing. She would never kiss a boy, never read a good book without the help of audio, and never even graduate from elementary school.

And if my Dad died, though he usually kept to himself in his office, I didn't know how I would cope. I lost my Mother by moving here, but losing my Dad too... It would be too much. I couldn't let anything happen to them. My protective instincts for my Sister kicked in and before I could think of a comeback, I blurted out something I couldn't believe I'd say.

"I will join the Ravens, if that's what it takes. But I want a guarantee my Sister and Dad are well." Heat rushed to my face; had I really said that? I agreed to something I knew nothing about, something that could cost me more than I knew.

But then, the other part of me thought I made the right decision, doing anything in my power to protect my Dad and Sister.

"Great, the Raven Master will start with you tomorrow," Sarah said, putting on a smug smile.

"Start what?" I asked.

"Your training. You need to train."

"When? I'm busy, you know."

"During school hours, after everyone is in class, we will send someone to get you, and you will come here for your training."

"What about my report card? And my Sister and Dad? Where do they fit into this?" I snapped, suddenly angry.

"They will get better, and once they are fully cured, everything will be normal for them. And don't worry about your grades, we'll see that you pass. That's all you need."

"I won't be participating in any trainings until I see my family up and around in our house with my own eyes."

"If you refuse to train, then we won't heal them."

"I will train, *after* I see my Sister and Dad walking."

"We'll see about that."

"It's time for our guest to leave. We will see her tomorrow," the cloaked figure said from the back.

"Do we need to blindfold her or knock her out or is her half-commitment enough?" Sarah asked him.

"Don't bother, she is capable of walking. Send a few people to escort her."

"If you tell anyone about this meeting, the deal

is off. Your family will die, and we'll hurt you in any way we can." Sarah gestured to a person behind me. Seconds later, my arms were released.

"Come on," my escort whispered to me. I got up and followed her out of the room. When we reached the exit door, I noticed it was the door that had the big *R* on it. She pushed it open, and we walked into the halls of my school.

"Wait. Wouldn't people see this door and wonder what's inside?" I asked.

"Humans can't see this door."

"And we aren't human?"

"We consider ourselves more than humans, better than them."

"Isn't that kind of, uh, insulting them?"

"Depends on how you look at it. I think it's more of stating a fact."

Already, I could tell sleeping would be impossible tonight.

CHAPTER FIVE

MARRY

I lay awake in bed, thinking how I shouldn't have agreed to whatever I agreed to. In fact, I don't even know what I agreed to. That's why I shouldn't have agreed. It could be a boot camp, or a spa.

The weird thing was, I was almost looking forward to the training tomorrow, or whatever it was. Knowing my Dad and Grant were going to be okay made the rest seem doable.

The worst part, though, was I didn't understand any of it. I wished everything was normal. My Sister and Dad at home, me feeding the horses; my life was perfect before we moved to this hellhole. Ugh.

Although it was 5 a.m., there was no chance of getting any more sleep, so I got up and made a nice breakfast. After making it, I realized what I'd made absentmindedly: blueberry and chocolate chip pancakes, exactly what my mother used to make on Sundays.

Looking at my plate, I cried. I missed Mom so, so much, I couldn't begin to describe the pain. I wished she was here to at least comfort me. I talked to her on Skype sometimes, but that's not nearly as good as seeing her in real life. And I tried to call her to let her know about Dad and Grant, but there was no answer. Maybe later after I stopped crying I'd try calling again, but I didn't need a babysitter. I needed my family.

I should have been nicer to her, spent more time with her. I didn't know anything that would have helped. Could I've gotten her to stay with Dad? I wondered if I would ever get over my mother being gone. I sighed as I rubbed the tears off my cheeks and then ate. Even with the painful memories in those pancakes, I had to eat; no use in wasting food.

The bus engine grinded gears as it took off toward school. My stop was the last, so I didn't waste much time. It took me straight to school. I wondered where Toby was. He wasn't on the bus. Was he skipping class? My mind spun. I had no clue what this day would bring. Would those people knock me out again? Or would they simply come get me? They said yesterday they would send someone, but that didn't mean someone wouldn't take me out in the process.

Also, what would they teach me? They said "training" and that didn't sound like sitting in a class memorizing flash cards. Maybe they would give some explanations, answer my questions.

I felt myself sweat, but was surprised when I wiped my forehead and felt liquid. By the time I was in class, my hands shook like crazy and I couldn't stop them.

That fierce ear ringing began again, and almost made me throw-up. But it disappeared as a teacher came to the door.

"Excuse me, is Marry here?" she asked my teacher.

"Yes, she's over there," my teacher said, motioning toward me. I didn't want to go. She came to me and pulled me off my chair. She was strong, too strong for an average person.

"You need to come with me. You know why."

My hands shook twice as much as before, and I thought my legs would give out as I left the room. The lady led me to the door with the R, and forced me inside.

"We're going to the second lowest floor where the Raven Master is waiting for you."

Wait, second to lowest floor? That meant this was under the school; how many floors were there?

It took a while to really take the place in, and when I did, I realized how beautiful it was. Nice red tile flooring and chocolate-brown walls, the doors were teddy bear tan. Together, it was beautiful. Whoever owned this was rich. My ears started ringing, but I tried to tune it out.

"Here we are," she said as she opened a door. I gasped. This had to be the biggest floor in the entire place. People roamed nearby as well as far away, but they weren't just walking and talking... they were fighting.

Combatants crouched in battle positions, each holding some sort of weapon, trying viciously to take down their opponent. I froze in the doorway. I did not want to go in. What if someone accidently punched me?

"Come on. Let's not keep him waiting." The lady grabbed my arm and pulled me along. I struggled for a moment, but stopped when I realized it was a lost cause; she must have been five times stronger than I was.

The room smelled of sweat, not so pleasant. I looked around and was again amazed. To my right was a mini-forest area with bushes, trees, and grassland that looked very, very real. To my left people fought with bloody fists and weapons. In front was a first aid station. I couldn't see past that, but I could only imagine what might be beyond. Finally, the annoying ear-ringing stopped, and I was at peace.

"Ah, there you are," a male said, walking toward us.

"Raven Master." My escort did a half-bow.

"Hello, Marry, my name is Joey Stansov." He shook my hand. I studied him; he looked to be in his early twenties.

"What am I doing here?" I asked.

"I'm going to tell you things about this place, and maybe about you. Come on." He walked toward the medic station. I followed obediently, and as we passed the triage, I noticed a few bull's eyes against a wall, with people shooting both arrows and guns. I shied away from them, and followed Joey to a bench.

"So, I'm thinking you want explanations," he said.

"Yeah, that would be helpful since I don't know what the hell is going on." I practically spat out the words.

"Don't interrupt 'til the end," he warned.

"Okay, I'll try."

"We are Ravens, and as long as you are in this compound, you are a Raven. Unless of course, you have evidence of being a Slayer, in which case, you would be dead - Fast."

I gaped at him. It was creepy having someone stalk me in my bedroom, but it was creepier having someone threaten me, especially when they meant it.

"The Ravens have magical powers, as in we can shapeshift and each person can summon a certain element- water, fire, earth or air. The Slayers have powers too; they can shoot electric blasts and have slightly enhanced stamina."

"Ha, ha. Very funny. 'Powers,' eh?"

"I'm serious. But no more talk about that." He waved his hand through the air as if brushing away a thought. "Okay, this might sound extremely weird and unbelievable, and may be harsh. But I don't know how else to say it, so I'm just gonna spit it out," Joey said.

"Wait. Before you say anything, how do you know my name?"

"I know your name, Marry Clad, because your mother told me the last time she came here."

"What do you mean? My mother is in Texas; she was born there and never left."

"I'm referring to your biological mother, who is gone. I'm sorry."

"Your wrong, my mother is in Texas and my father is in the hospital here."

"Marry, they adopted you when you were a baby, and swore they would never tell you about yourself or the Ravens - us. It's horrible, I know. And I don't agree with what they did."

I refused to hear it; they wouldn't keep

something like this from me, would they? But if it was true, did they even really love me? Did they know this? Was Joey lying? He must be. This was just a question of who I trusted more, Joey or my Mom and Dad. That wasn't even a question.

But what if my Mom broke up with my Dad on purpose, convincing him to take me here - right into the Raven's hands. She made it look like a coincidence brilliantly if that was the case.

"You're wrong," I whispered.

"I'm sorry you had to find out this way. I sort of thought you knew." His voice was filled with sympathy, but I didn't know if it was an act or real. Could it be possible what he was saying was true?

"How was I supposed to know? Who would tell me? Even if my true parents are dead, I don't even know their names," I suddenly snapped. A medical tray fell off a table near us, and Joey stared at it for a moment before continuing.

"They were alive. They were wonderful warriors, probably the reason we won the fight they died in. I'm sorry, what happened to her was a tragedy. I can still see your mother dancing around the battlefield."

"What? Battlefield dancing?" That made no sense.

"Never mind. I'm sorry you had to find out this way."

"Why didn't they tell me? And why do you keep apologizing?"

57

"They wanted to protect you from your future. It was bound to happen anyway, but they wanted to avoid it as long as possible. They wanted you to have a normal life."

"Why would they lie to me? They've said over and over how lucky they were to have me, and now you're saying they aren't my real parents." Sadness swept through me, and I felt tears in my eyes. I believed them to have always told me the truth, and they always did... didn't they? "I trusted them." I knew I shouldn't believe Joey when he said they were dead, but what he said felt true.

He wanted me to think that my Sister and Dad weren't even blood related to me. I always wondered why I didn't get any of my Mom's beautiful features, why I looked nothing like my relatives.

"They were good people," Joey said softly.

"This is too much information at once. I need to leave. As much as I hate to say it, I would come back willingly... I guess."

Joey seemed hesitant, like a part of him wanted to let me go, but another part told him to make me stay. "Please," I pleaded. It took a second more for him to decide, but when he did, I could tell he wasn't about to change his mind.

"You can leave, but not to your house. We have empty rooms on the first floor. You can go there for a while, or if you prefer a public lounge, that's open too. I have to do some things. When I'm done I'll come get you."

"Thank you," I breathed, utterly relieved. He turned and flashed me a smile, something that seemed rare.

"Come on, I will show you where you can stay."

CHAPTER SIX

MARRY

Why did life have to be this hard? I mean, seriously, sometimes it seemed like the world was against me; trying to make my life miserable, and I wasn't sure I could take much more. This was the worst yet - being told my Mom and Dad were a lie might as well be child abuse.

I sat on the floor of my destroyed dorm room, sobbing my eyeballs out. It was such a deep pain, a stabbing throbbing pain against my chest worse than any cut. Knowing my Mom and Dad valued their oaths over me made me shudder.

I looked up from my hands, and processed the damage I had done to the room. The kitchen chairs were all tipped, glass was on the ground from a flower pot that had been on the table, the sheets and bedding from the bed were thrown onto the ground, my fan was spinning wildly, and I had multiple cuts on my feet bleeding through my socks. But none of that mattered, it was my parents who mattered, real and fake alike. It was all too much, I couldn't handle it.

Suddenly, getting a knife and cutting myself didn't seem like such a bad idea. In fact, it seemed like a great idea; I could bleed out all the pain inside me. I scrambled into the kitchenette, not bothering to avoid broken glass in the process, and grabbed a knife from the drawer. The blade hovered over my wrist. My hand shook so violently. I felt the tip scratch my wrist. Would cutting myself ease the ache in my chest? Physical pain for mental pain... right?

I dragged the knife up my arm, the cold metal digging into my soft flesh and slicing it open. A thin line of red liquid followed behind the blade. At first, I didn't feel anything, but after a couple seconds of shock, fire shot up my forearm.

I cried out, and dropped the knife. That was a deeper cut than I'd ever done before. The knife fell onto my other wrist, gouging a deep hole with the tip. This pain seized my breath, squeezed my lungs from taking in air. But one good thing, it was working. My mental pain was fading.

Joey burst through the door. His blue eyes scanned the room, and when he saw me shock crossed his face, though he swiftly shook it off and put on his stoic face.

"What are you doing? Stop!" he yelled, running over to me. The cold floor tile felt good on my bare legs and hands, but once it warmed, it wasn't nice anymore. Joey crouched beside me, snatching up my bleeding arm.

"I didn't realize you took it so hard. I shouldn't have left you alone." He moved my arm so he could see the cuts. More sobs came to my throat, not because of my mother or father, but from shame and embarrassment for what I did to the room and myself, it—and I—was wrecked.

"What have I done?" I whispered.

"Nothing, you have done nothing except hurt yourself. The room's damage doesn't matter. We need to get you to a Follower, hopefully they'll help. Can you walk?" he asked. I motioned towards my socks and groaned. He nodded, seeing the slits and the blood coming through them.

"Okay, I'm carrying you, then."

I just nodded. Even saying okay seemed to take too much effort. I felt dizzy, from blood loss or imagination, I didn't know. Joey didn't hesitate; he swept me into his arms, and hurried out of the room.

The first - no, second thing I noticed was how muscular he was. The first was how much my feet and arms hurt. I closed my eyes, unable to keep them open, and listened to Joey's heart beating fast and strong.

I woke in a room that resembled a hospital room, Joey staring down at me with concern in his eyes. I turned away, suddenly reminded of my stinging cuts. Joey had ripped cloth from something and wrapped it around my arm, trying to stop the bleeding, but the thin fabric was soaked in blood. I cringed, glancing at the mess of blood on my lap.

"What do you want me to say?" Joey asked, cutting the silence.

I worked several seconds to find my voice. "W—what do you mean?"

"We can hardly say you cut yourself and trashed your room because you found out your parents adopted you."

"What does it matter, now."

His lips pressed to a line. "I'll say you and I were training and I scraped you a bit, as for your foot cuts... I will just say you broke a window with your foot. Not far from the truth. This is only if they ask, hopefully they won't bother."

"Mm-k," I said, my voice shook, as I tried my best to hide the pain. I let my head fall into my hands. Why did I even care? I was alone, had no one.

"Hey. What's your favorite color?" he asked casually. I looked at him, his blue eyes already watching me.

Totally puzzled from such an off-the-wall question, I said, "Red."

"Cool," he said, bobbing his head and looking at anything but me.

There was a pause, and then I asked, "What's yours?"

"Green." He watched the - what did he call them? Followers? - as she hustled through the door. We sat in silence waiting for her to do her thing. Joey turned to me, and I thought I saw a bit of genuine affection in his eyes, but maybe I was imagining it.

"Are you feeling okay?" Joey asked.

"Yeah, I'm fine, considering." A minute passed.

"Hey, did I tell you much about Followers?"

"Uh. You haven't told me anything." *Except what I didn't need to hear.*

"The person who is going to heal you is a Follower. Followers have two main abilities, one can heal people, another can make things appear or sound differently than they actually do. The reason we don't use guns is because it takes a lot of powerful Followers to make a gunshot sound like something else," he said. "You can always tell them apart from Ravens and Slayers because they are less bulky and don't have as much muscle. They also tend to have thin hair and are tall."

"*Heal* people? Like with herbs or medicine?"

"No, no, like with magic. You'll see. As soon as you get healed."

"With *magic*? What the hell?"

"Just wait. You'll see."

It took forever for the Follower to get ready, but it was probably only a couple minutes. She gave my cuts a disapproving look.

"I will heal them, but be more careful next time. It gets difficult to heal everyone by the end of the day, using so much magic gets kind of tiring. The less people who get hurt, the easier my job is." The lady was clearly annoyed.

For a moment, I thought Joey was going to say something like "also, can you heal her mind?" or "do you know where a mental hospital is?" but all he said was, "She also has cuts on her feet, if you haven't seen those." The lady groaned and looked at my feet. As if clarifying she saw the cuts, she groaned a second time, a little louder. I pretended not to hear, because I wasn't sure how I was supposed to react, although I heard her loud and clear.

Looking at Joey, I saw him ignoring her too, unless of course, he didn't, in fact, hear her groan, which I doubted. She closed her eyes, touching one of my feet with each hand. At first I thought she was meditating or something, but when I felt what could only be described as energy run through me, I knew she was doing much more.

I felt a strange itchy feeling on the bottom of my feet, and then the lady opened her eyes and came up to my arms, resting a hand on the one I cut. When I felt that tingle run through me again, I promptly brought my gaze to the cuts on my arm. The cuts started to fill in with flesh and skin, rising from the deepest part of the cut to be level with the rest of my arm. I gasped, and lightly touched where the slice used to be, the new skin felt the same as everywhere else, if not a little smoother.

"Thank you," Joey said. I gazed at my now-healed cuts and touched them, just to make sure they were really healed.

"Look, it's almost past school hours, people might start looking for you. Want me to show you the way to the classrooms?" Joey asked.

"Yes. Getting out of here would be great," I said. Joey didn't look into my eyes for the entire walk back. When I slipped into the school, I found my place in science, although it was half over.

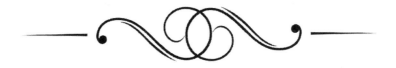

I lingered around math class the next day,

pretending to be getting ready for English when a teacher came to get me. "Marry, come with me. Joey says he needs to talk with you, and you need to train. Yesterday you barely got anything done."

I sighed. I knew this was coming, Joey had told me. But I didn't know it would be so early. I was actually hoping to try for an A on my English report card. Guess that idea was out.

"Lead the way," I murmured. She walked away, obviously knowing I would follow, and led me to one of the doors with an *R* on it.

Inside the training room, the air conditioner was cranked. The smell of sweat and fire filled the air, and I wondered what was burning, or why it smelt like smoke inside. People everywhere sparred with swords or practiced their aim with a bow. I watched as I was led to Joey, praying nobody would get hurt, especially if there was blood. I'd had enough of blood at that point.

"Finally, school geek returns," Joey said playfully as he came up to me.

"I'm not a school geek. I wanted to try to get *something* that resembles an A or B on my report card. Grade 11 matters for college."

"Oh, so maybe nerd is a better name?"

I glared at him, and he laughed dryly, but it didn't reach his eyes.

"Okay, but I *actually* have things to tell you. And things to do," Joey said, motioning for me to join him on the bench.

"Why is everyone fighting? Just for practice?"

"That about sums it up. They are fighting each other since they can't just stroll into the Slayers' compound and try out their skills on them. More fun, but much more dangerous."

"The Slayers' compound? Who are they? And how can it be fun to hurt them? That's just sick."

"They are like, I don't know, our rival, I guess? That's who we fight, why we train, and things like that. They say the god that blessed them is the rival of the god who blessed us, and we don't exactly agree with how they do things. What I'm saying is if you see a giant building that says *Slayers*, try not to get too close if you can avoid it. But if you do happen to get captured, remember you have some sort of magical power, and if you can figure out how to access it, you'll be able to escape."

"Oh."

"You probably won't see a building like that, but be careful. If you do go in the Slayers building, and they figure out you are a Raven, they won't hesitate to kill you."

"How delightful," I grunted.

"I'm serious. They will kill you. They hate us."

"Why do you guys hate each other so much you have to kill them to find peace? It must be something pretty serious."

"When we were sent to this earth, things happened. It also might be the way we train. But they have nothing to say about that. Some people say it's just instinct—that the gods altered our thoughts to make us resort to fighting. We're like their little army. The Slayers don't even let you stay awake past their 'bed time' at like nine o'clock. No parties, no fun, no nothing."

"I don't think I'll find the training that bad." He raised his eyebrows. I immediately corrected myself. "Don't get it in your head I'm going to like it, 'cause I don't think I will. But I don't think it's going to be *terrible*." I emphasized on the last word. Because I really *didn't* want him to think I liked it.

"Anyway, we are going to practice fighting, physically instead of just talking about it and watching other people."

"What? I can't fist fight you! I might hurt you or someone else in this room." I looked at Joey as he made a face. "What?"

"We practice every single day with swords, fists, anything we have against each other, preparing for a day someone might come into the compound to kill us. I think it's kind of funny for you to be concerned about hurting me or someone else in the room." He seemed amused with our conversation. "You have to do it sometime, or I can guarantee you will die, or get captured," Joey said, prompting me to get up.

"Dude, I guarantee I'll die, and you'll die, and everyone in this room will die. Death is the only point of life. It's just how you'll die that changes."

He grinned. "Right, whatever. But you do have to learn to fight sometime."

"Fine, but I actually need to know *how* to throw my fist and make it hurt my opponent more than me," I said. Joey laughed.

"Yeah, I was actually planning on getting you to punch a brick wall without even knowing how, and without gloves," he said sarcastically, laughing, but again, it didn't quite reach his eyes.

CHAPTER SEVEN

MARRY

I lunged for him, striking out with my hands bunched into fists. He jumped to the side, dodging my dig and jumping onto my foot. I managed to land a punch and he grunted, but not for one second did he let his guard down. I couldn't believe I was doing this. What if I hurt him?

"You're being sloppy. Make your blows precise, like chopping up a jelly bean." Joey said.

"Like chopping a jelly bean?"

"Well, yeah. 'Cause they are small and hard to cut. You getting it? You gotta be precise to cut a jelly bean."

"Okay. Whatever," I said. Joey chuckled. I lunged at him again, this time planning it out a bit. I didn't punch him first this time, waiting for him to kick me - which he usually did opposed to punching -   and when he did, I caught his foot and yanked it back with everything I had. Joey fell to the ground, scrambling to get himself back up, meanwhile punching out with his fist, effectively keeping me from pinning him. He swung at me from his crouched position on the ground, and instead of dodging I grabbed his fist in an attempt to knock him off balance, but failed. He stood in one motion, using the momentum from his punch.

"Shouldn't have done that. You helped me up. You're trying to keep me down, remember?"

"You don't think I saw that? Lesson learned. Don't grab your opponent's fist if they are on the ground already."

"Good," he said, striking his fist into my stomach, me being too unfocused by our little chit-chat to block it. I stumbled backward, clutching my middle. I staggered, unable to strike at Joey because of the pain distracting me.

"Dammit. Pause. I can't fight you when I'm hurt."

"And if I was a Slayer? What then? They wouldn't stop when you simply said pause. Deal with the pain. You would have to in a real fight. People *want* you dead. That's why you need to kill them first. Course, try not to kill me, please.

You'll be fine." I glanced up, and saw he didn't stop, jumping towards me and flinging his fist through the air towards my jaw. I dodged it just in time, afterward flinging my own fist at *his* jaw. Of course, like almost always, I didn't hit him. *Jeez, he's way too experienced.*

"Come on. You can do better than that. Can't you?" he mocked, and I glared at him.

"I'm not the one who's been doing this for years. This is my first time, unlike you and your friends here." I nodded towards a group of people, all fighting.

"That's true; I guess you're doing pretty good if I consider that," he said. "Hey, do you think you're ready for a weapon?" he asked, and raised his hand for us to stop. I stopped.

"A weapon?" I asked, disbelief cursing through me, even though I saw people using swords and such. "As in, swords and flails and stuff?"

"Yes. I told you already, Slayers will want to kill you. You can kill them faster with weapons."

"Why not guns?" I asked, noticing how none of the people training used them.

"We use guns sometimes, but we don't give them out freely. Mostly because, as I said, it's hard for Followers to mask the sound. And if random humans saw our abilities, that could be a disaster. Not to mention how annoying they are," he said. "Also, this place isn't weird - it's more like dangerous."

"Dangerous? I thought you said it was safe.

And I do believe you, by the way, even though I probably shouldn't."

"You have no reason not to believe me, and yes, I did say it was safe, I think, but that was only to get you to come."

"Ha ha, very funny, can't even believe you came up with that. And I also have no reason to believe you," I mocked.

"It's not a joke, Marry. Now, do you want to choose a weapon?"

"Guess I'm going to have to - you'll make me even if I don't want to. Am I right?"

"Pretty much. Come on." He walked towards a door with a big *R* on it in the corner of the room. I followed, like expected.

"Don't freak out," he said as he opened the door. I peered inside, and didn't like what I saw. There were knives and axes and swords and flails and every other violent thing I could think of lining the walls and piled on shelves. I took a deep breath, and tried to listen to Joey. He walked in and picked up a normal sword, probably not his favorite weapon.

"Pick something, anything, and I will help you use it like a civilized person would."

"I don't think you would be considered 'civilized' if you're using a deadly weapon to kill other people."

"Yeah, yeah, just pick something, hurry up."

I stepped inside the room, cautiously, and looked around on the shelves. I wasn't too big on axes or swords, but one thing did catch my attention.

"Can I use this?" I asked, lifting a beautiful staff and examining it. The dark wood tangled around itself, working its way to the top, and there it embraced a white stone that seemed to glow. It looked almost alive. The wood was hard under my fingertips, and it seemed more fitting than a cold metal sword.

"Staffs are very difficult to use, and take a lot of skill, maybe you should try a sword or something first."

"I'm not using a sword."

"Are you sure you want the staff? You could use a bow or something instead."

"Yeah, no. This is the only thing in this room that doesn't look like a death weapon. Not that this isn't a death weapon."

"Fine, I guess after a while you could learn how to use that thing. Maybe." He shrugged. "Come on." He walked out of the room, and I followed.

"Aren't we going to like fight each other or something?" I asked. He positioned himself opposite me.

"Not yet, first you need to know how to even hit me with that." He nodded towards my staff. "Try something on me, anything. All I will do is block. Try to hit me." I hesitated; not wanting to hurt him, but then I probably won't even hit him. I lunged and tried to strike at his stomach, hoping to knock him back. It was shaky and awkward, and he deflected it with his sword effortlessly, almost looking bored. I tried again for several minutes to hit him, but gave up.

"Okay, I get your point. Where do I aim and how do I hit?" I asked.

"You need to hold it properly first." He studied my hold, which was awkward and weird.

"You're right handed?" he asked.

"Yeah."

"Okay. Start with your right hand on the top, and your left a bit below it." I did what he said, adjusting a little.

"Also, twist your left hand a bit to the right; it's facing the wrong way."

"Yeah, yeah," I grunted.

"Hey, you're the one who wanted to use that stupid thing. Don't complain."

I sighed, and we stood in silence for a moment.

"Now just move it a bit, get used to how it moves around."

I carried it over my shoulder and twisted it around; all the moves were straight forward when you held it the right way.

"So you pretty much have freedom with how you do the moves, but there are a few good places to aim for."

"Mm-k, where?"

"If you get the chance, hit your opponent's head, but the knuckles and knees are good places to aim for. Also the collarbone or hips, but they might be difficult to hit. Then if you're really desperate, you could try to hit the arms," he said. I didn't warn him when I tried to hit him, but he seemed like he was already ready for it. I sighed in exasperation when he blocked it effortlessly, and he laughed.

"You need to do better than that to fool me. Try to fake hit my legs, then actually hit my arms. Also, please don't aim for my head," he said. I laughed, and tried again to hit him, doing what he suggested. I mostly failed, but I did tap him for a second before he pushed it away with his sword. Here and now, I realized how easy it was to forget he was blackmailing me.

"You're getting a bit better, but it still needs work. Lots of work."

"Thanks for the reassurance."

Joey smiled that annoying little smile he always put on when I was angry.

CHAPTER EIGHT

MARRY

Walking through Los Angeles toward the hospital was really quite relaxing. Apart from the uncomfortably hot temperature and stench of pollution, the busy city was quite nice. Something about watching the people go about their busy lives was interesting.

I turned down a less populated alley, following a shortcut I saw on Google Maps earlier and getting out of the intense sun. There was hardly anybody in this alley, and the few people I did see seemed to be writing graffiti or just passing through like I was. My ears started ringing, and I rubbed them.

I started to feel funny - I wasn't sure exactly how to explain it, sort of like I was being watched, I guess. I swore I heard footsteps fall in step with mine, but when I looked back, nobody was there. Someone coughed and I jumped, whipping my head around. I relaxed when I saw it was only one of the guys drawing graffiti and turned back to the path I was on.

Upon hearing steps from behind me, I turned to see a tall buff man stomping along. His dread-locked hair was pulled up in a ponytail, and he looked old, like around forty. I smiled at him in an attempt to make my looking back less awkward, and he just glared. I scooted against the wall, out of his way, and pulled out my phone with the Google map up.

A hand clasped around my arm and I yelped. The dreadlocked guy yanked me into his arms and bolted down the sidewalk. Screaming at the top of my lungs, I squirmed in his grasp, trying to kick or punch or hurt him in any way possible. His body was like steel; no matter how hard I struggled or how much I tried to kick, his grasp didn't loosen.

"Oh, my dear girl, you're a fighter, I see." He laughed, as if my attempt was no more than a joke. His German accent rung through my ears. "My tribe likes little girls like you."

"Let me go!" I screamed, wishing more than

anything that someone sane was walking through this alley. Someone who could call nine-one-one.

"But, my girl, if I take you with me I could be rich or the most favored man in my tribe. Depending on what I do with you, of course." He laughed again, as if this was a huge joke.

"You're not taking me to whatever 'tribe' you're talking about! I won't go!" I continued trying to bite and kick and punch, anything I could think of.

"You're already going, my girl. And I'm already rich and favored," he purred, swinging an arm to my head, knocking my world to black.

Everything swirled around me. I didn't know where I was. At home, half-awake, half-asleep? I closed my eyes, willing the conscious part of me back to sleep. I was exhausted. I felt grass and dirt under my nails, so how could this be home?

A cool breeze ruffled my hair, bringing the tangy scent of pine trees and moist earth. Chirping overhead reminded me of birds gathered around the feeder at home. Then the stench of burning flesh and hot electricity stung my nose, making me want to throw-up. Where was I and how did I get here?

Suddenly, it all came back in a flash. I snapped my eyes open, blinking a few times to make the world stop spinning, but it didn't fully stop, and my vision was blurry.

Flickers of blue electric-looking zaps flew into a lion darting through the trees. Wait, he was only half lion. What? I squinted. Yep, the creature was half lion, half human, and most definitely some sort of electricity flowed into him, in shots like a laser weapon might inflict. Was there such a thing as a laser gun? He dodged many of the attacks, ducking behind thick brush. Others hit him, knocking him over, taking out newborn foliage. He ran in the opposite direction to us - probably trying to flee.

I whipped around to where the charges were coming from, the world spun once more, but what I thought I saw was not a weapon with electricity shooting out, but a hand.

I blinked. Two females, each with tiny lightning bolts flowing out of their fingertips. They were in tight uniforms that hugged their chests and legs; it looked like fighting gear.

I fell to the ground, my head wanted to split open.

At the edge of the grassy clearing, a cougar and a tiger bounded around nearby bush, running toward the lion. Wait... a tiger? I didn't think they lived around here. I stared in awe as my vision cleared. The two animals mauled and killed the lion.

I crawled, scuttling backward, afraid of the cougar quickly approaching me. Catching a root, I stumbled over my own feet, falling onto my back.

The cougar stopped in its tracks, and stared at me. It looked rather unnatural. The tiger trotted up beside the cougar, after ripping the lion's face apart, though. The cougar glanced at the two women and it seemed to set them off.

One of the women shot electric shocks, which they - the cougar and tiger - dodged easily. The other lady pulled out a magnificent shining blade, the white handle glinting in the dim light, and positioned herself in front of the woman with the magic.

Wait, did I really consider it magic? Out of the corner of my eye, I saw a flicker of black and a rustle of bushes. A man in all black leaped toward me. Survival instincts kicked in and I grabbed a knife I'd never seen before sheathed to my ankle.

I scrambled to my feet as his foot snaked out and hit my side, making me lose my balance but I thankfully stayed upright. My side burned, but I pushed the pain away. Huh, seemed Joey helped me learn a *bit* of fighting skill.

I jumped away from him, giving myself some time. He was tall and his hair was messy, but extremely thin. Maybe he was a Follower, if what Joey said was correct, but why would a Follower fight? No time to think about that. I tried to remember everything Joey told me to do when attacking with a blade. Damn, I could barely recall any of it.

I darted to the side, and slashed the man in the arm, not very deep, but it would maybe distract him. I hated hurting him, and it took every ounce of my willpower to tell myself he was evil and it was okay to hurt him. He grunted, but other than that, had no reaction. Then the cut healed itself, right before my eyes.

"Dammit, you *are* a bloody Follower." Of course he could heal himself. I was so screwed. He was practically invincible! I would have to kill him in one blow, before he got a chance to heal himself. I couldn't do it. Kill an innoce - wait, he wasn't innocent... fine, I couldn't bring myself to kill a person, innocent or not. But I had to. I had to keep telling myself that, or... well, I didn't want to know what would happen, but it wouldn't be good.

He smiled at my reaction, and jumped toward me, kicking me, yet again, on my side. I yelped, and my body filled with a rage I couldn't control, much less had ever seen in myself before. My gut twisted.

My hands crinkled up, sprouting fur and sharp claws; my back and head *moved*. The searing pain laced through me. My shredded clothing and knife lay on the ground before me, and I was suddenly much shorter.

The man was on top of me before I could

figure out how to use all my new limbs properly, but fortunately, I felt an uncanny familiarity with this new creature. I jumped out of the way of his knife hurdling toward my face and leaped higher and farther than I thought possible. My back legs propelled me into the air, driving me toward the enemy.

The man positioned the knife so I'd land on it, right in my heart, but one of my front paws wacked it away like a fly without me even telling myself to do it. My vision seemed enhanced, and I could feel every stitch of the man's clothing beneath my paws as I pushed him to the ground.

Seemingly of their own accord, my paws twisted his head until a crack rang out. I backed away, panting. It was like I could *smell* my success hanging in the air. I looked at the tiger and cougar, suddenly hyperaware of their presence, *sensing* their needs and wants in my mind.

The tiger wanted more action, and the cougar was desperate for something. They'd taken down their opponents, and were looking in my direction, taking slow, silent steps towards me.

I growled, and hunched down, in the perfect pouncing position, and slowly backed toward the deeper forest. They kept coming, moving toward me. I glanced over my shoulder and saw a thick healthy tree, if I could climb it - which I knew in my new form I could - I might be able to stay up there for a while.

I made my move, pivoting on my hind legs,

launching myself into the air. Going almost completely parallel with the tree, my back claws dug into the bark while my paws and head rotated, aiming for the closest branch. I did it effortlessly. A pang of surprise ran through the cougar, so strong it resonated through to me.

I thought the tiger was jealous, but it was hard to tell. Crouching on the branch, I prepared to pounce if they were to come up. After a moment of them edging closer, I realized my fear and anger wasn't for them.

It was me trying to soothe my own fear. Being so violent and killing another person set me off, not to mention that I'd shifted into some four-legged critter, a big critter no less. I wasn't keeping it together. I glanced around, making sure nobody else came at me. With my better vision, I saw a rustle of bushes and a glimpse of blue.

When I concentrated on the spot, I heard panting. Someone was there, good guy or bad?

I could almost see the cougar's mind working, deciding. It nodded to the tiger, and stepped into thick bushes with the person still hiding. I expected a scream or the sound of a throat being ripped out, but I didn't hear anything except a faint grunt from the cougar that turned into a human whimper.

After a few moments of rustling in the bushes, a man my age, walked out. I squinted at him, and it took a moment to recognize him as Joey. I breathed a sigh of relief. His presence was calming. I relaxed my position, but then realized he might think I was a threat, since there was no way he would know I was the animal in the tree - I didn't even know what animal I was - unless... was Joey the cougar? I felt again for the cougar's needs, but felt a big nothing.

"Marry," Joey breathed, holding out his hand for me, "it's Joey. Do you know how to switch back into human form?"

That problem never occurred to me, much less being stuck like this. A pierce of fear, cold and thick stabbed through me. What if I couldn't turn back? All I managed was a whimper, and a lowering of my head and pawing of the bark. Joey sighed.

"It's okay. You'll be able to switch. It's easy. I was the cougar, and the tiger is Sarah," he said, confirming my thoughts. "Although, I'd request you come down so you don't go into human form and fall off that branch you're on." I hesitated a moment, then jumped down, landing on the ground with barely a thump.

"Okay, imagine yourself as Marry, not the leopard you are. Imagine your thick, wavy brown hair." I growled; like I didn't know what I looked like. I could picture myself without help. "Okay, I get it. Sorry. But when you have the picture, wish to become it. It should work."

I focused on myself, envisioning my ugly brown hair in contrast with my light skin, and my bright green eyes that stuck out like the first leaves in the spring. And lastly, my slender build making my body small, but also making my muscled arms more visible than I would have liked.

The feeling of my body shifting into another form was not pleasant, not even a little. The excruciating pain filled all my nerves. The skin and fur of my former leopard body folded in on itself, tearing away from the fresh human skin underneath. My muscles pulled and ordered themselves to take human form, at which point I could no longer hear, feel, or sense the other animals.

I looked at my hands and flexed them, making them into fists and then parting them. I felt a wash of relief that I was able to get back to normal, but then a tingle of exposure. I felt blind with only human senses.

"I'm a freaking cat! An animal!" I said in horror, sitting on the cold ground. I looked at Joey; he met my gaze.

"You should get clothing on first. Markus, come out and give Sarah's to Marry." I flushed, realizing I had no attire on. Joey glanced at the tiger, still watching, and said, "Stay as a tiger, Sarah, you can run with us then come out when we get to the city. We'll buy you something to wear. Also, in case you were wondering, Marry, you're a white and orange leopard."

The tiger growled, but remained a tiger. I absorbed all that happened, and my mind turned to stone. I sucked in a sharp breath. "But – you

- what did - those people - what did they - the electricity - their hands were -" I shuddered.

"Stop, we'll talk about it tomorrow," Joey said.

"You – you - You *killed* them - I mean - they're *dead*. How - how did they - that blue stuff..." Markus came out of the bush. He had dirty blond hair that fell about to his ears, styled like he just got out of bed. He managed to make it look good on him. It seemed weird to think he could have helped a murderer. His eyes were blue and green, and when he smiled, he showed lots of teeth. He tossed me the clothes, and both boys turned and waited for me to dress. I yanked on the pants and shirt as fast as I could with my trembling hands, and gave Markus and Joey the okay to turn back around. I opened my mouth to say something, but Joey cut me off.

"Hold your questions or concerns. Tomorrow, we'll talk about it."

"That's the problem. I don't *want* to talk about it! I don't even feel safe in my own house!"

"If you want to stay at the compound tonight, by all means. We have food and beds; you won't starve. Markus, heal her."

I blinked. I hadn't even considered staying there. In fact, it was a tempting offer. At least I might be safe there, even if some part of me was screaming these people are the ones who killed three innocent people—well, one wasn't, but two were.

"You look quite pale," Markus said as he came

up, but I wasn't paying much attention to him. I did want one thing in return for staying at the Raven place, though.

"I-I will stay at the compound, but - but only if - you come to the hospital with me – a -actually, not with me, just - just drop me - drop me off then wait - wait for me. I'll only be- be a while, I just - just want to - check on my Sis - actually, you kno - know who I want to see. A-also uh, could you - could you send someone - t-to feed my animals on the f-farm?" I could barely talk in full sentences I was so shocked by what happened.

Joey thought about it.

"Not a problem. You can talk to them while Markus and I get clothes for Sarah. I'll make sure your animals get fed." I coughed weakly, and it turned into a heave. I doubled over and vomited the remaining food from the day, hating the foul feel of puking more than turning into a leopard. I coughed out the last of it. Markus stared at me.

"My - my leg - Markus missed - missed my leg - it hurts," I said, trying to still my trembling hands. "Al - also, do you have - have any water - I'm thirsty I - I - I need water -" Joey took a deep breath and came over to me, putting a hand on my shoulder.

"You have to calm down, you're in shock," he said calmly. "Markus, come and see if her leg is hurt, then heal it."

"I'm not - not in shock - I, I - I think I just need - need water – please."

92

"You are in shock. Listen, you're going to the hospital to see your family. If you're still in shock by then we'll ask for help. We just need to make sure you'll be okay, which you will, but we need to take precautions. We'll make sure you're comfortable. If you need anything just tell me, okay?"

"O - okay. I need - need some - some water - I'm really thirsty."

"We don't have any water. You're not actually thirsty; your mind is imagining it," Joey said. My head pounded, and I couldn't think straight.

"Imagining it - just imagining - okay." I ran my hands over my face, trying to come to my senses. I couldn't even talk normally.

"Remember to breathe; we don't need you to pass out. Deep breaths, remember. Inhale, exhale." He was so calm, I found it surprising he could be this relaxed after killing people. Joey drew away his hand and stepped back.

"Where - where are - we anyway?" I asked, looking around carefully, making sure my eyes avoided the corpses Joey and Sarah killed. Joey thought for a moment.

"We're in *Angeles National Forest*." I glanced around, and instantly regretted it. Four bodies lay limp on the ground, two women, the man who tried to capture me, and one other. My eyes widened. I drew in a breath as my eyes ventured to the blood saturating the ground around them. If Markus hadn't been behind me with his hand on my mouth, blocking the scream before it happened, I would've lit up the area.

"Shhh. It's all right. Don't scream. There's a path people hike not too far away. The humans might get frightened." His voice was gentle, and I felt the steady way his chest rose and fell when he breathed. He saw I wasn't going to scream anymore, and delicately removed his hand from my mouth, his fingers lingering on my shoulder for a second before he stepped back. Weird how gentle someone who killed other people could be. I hadn't realized I was holding my breath until I gasped for air. I tried to cover it by coughing. Joey looked at me sideways, and my cheeks warmed.

"C'mon then, you two - I mean three. We have some hiking to do before we get back to civilization. This little scene will make a good news broadcast. If the Followers don't get here first."

CHAPTER NINE

MARRY

"H - how are you feeling?" I asked my father, pulling over a chair and taking his hand. He turned his head toward me - he was getting better, just very, *very* slowly - and smiled softly.

"I'm fine, would be finer if they let me go home," he whispered. *Always protecting me*, I thought. Even saying he was fine when he clearly wasn't. I couldn't bring myself to tell him I was involved with the Ravens when he looked so weak and helpless, so he remained oblivious that I knew his secrets. I smiled for my father's sake.

"I'm - I'm glad - to hear it."

"How's your Sister?" he asked.

"She's doing good," I said smiling, although it was part lie since she was doing as well as he was. Which was only a little better.

"That's great."

"So. How've the n - nurses been treating you?"

"They're nice. At least friendly." He smiled at me weakly. "However, I am lookin' forward to gettin' out of here."

"Well, of course, you are. The stench is enough to make me run for miles." He laughed quietly. "Dad, I'm so glad you're okay. That last time I came... For those moments I thought you were gone, I didn't know what to do. All I could think was there was nothing if you weren't here. I love you, Dad."

He sighed. "I love you too, hun. And I'm glad I'm not dead, but I'd give my life for you or Grant. In a heartbeat, no question." When I didn't say anything, he let his eyes close and his breathing became steady. I slipped my hand from his grasp and left the room, heading for the children's floor. Since Grant started doing better, she got moved onto the children's floor where all the other kids were.

The empty halls of the children's floor of the hospital were eerily silent as I came to my Sister's room, peeking my head inside to see her asleep. I walked in as quietly as I could, grabbing a chair on my way, sitting next to the bed. I gently took my Sister's hand from her stomach, careful to avoid touching the IV in her hand.

Grant was so peaceful when she slept, her breathing so, so steady. I imagined what kind of dreams she was having, probably nice and happy, whereas mine were pretty much nightmares. I shivered at the recollection of them. Grant stirred, and I looked to see her big blue eyes were watching me curiously. I smiled down at her.

"I didn't wake you up, did I?" I asked her.

"Hi, Marryyy," she exclaimed, more quiet than I would have liked. I squeezed her hand.

"I don't suppose you'd tell me how you're feeling?" I asked playfully.

"I'm not feeling great, but much, MUCH better than before." A grin split her face. Grant seemed to be feeling much better than my Dad was.

"It's kind of weird how I *never* have to eat or drink. I always expect to start feeling hungry in the morning, but just never do," she said. "The doctors say it's because they have all the food I need going straight into my belly," she pointed to her stomach "without me even needing to eat it!"

"That's pretty cool," I said. "In fact, I'm pretty hungry myself. I wish I had something like you have that would feed me without needing to actually put it in my mouth."

She scowled. "You don't really. I kind of miss eating. Well, unless I had to eat Dad's so-called soup. I think that stuff is poisoned," she said. I laughed, and she giggled a little. Someone pushed the door open and stuck their head in. The nurse looked at me.

"Fifteen minutes until visiting hours are done." She eased the door shut. Grant scowled.

"Darn grown-ups. They always ruin all the fun." She glared. I laughed more. Grant always seemed to crack me up.

"Not all the time! Remember Aunt Chloe? She was fun," I said.

"You're right. I remember her. She was *soooo* much fun. She'd even play with us!"

I nodded, giggling with her. "Well, I'm gonna head down then. Sorry 'bout the short visit, pumpkin."

"It's all riiiiight. Bye, sister!" She smiled.

I ruffled her hair as I turned away, and by the time I got to the door I heard faint noises of Grant's audio book playing. I smiled to myself. She was turning out like Mom, always reading a book.

The food in the downstairs cafeteria tasted stale and poorly made, but I still ate it. What else was I to eat? A man with a tray full of food sat next to me and almost instantly ignored the food, turning to me.

"What's making you so anxious?" he asked. It took a second to process his words, and when I did, I realized I was anxious. I didn't even know my own feelings until he told me.

"How do you know I'm feeling anxious?" I asked him. He made a face.

"Everyone can see it. Your hand is bunched up, you look like you're going to puke, and you haven't stopped frowning. By the way, my name is David Mann," he said, and smiled. "So, what's got under your skin, girl?" He sounded innocent enough, although I didn't know why he cared if I was anxious or not. I inched away from him.

"Umm. Everything is just so weird, and my friends - " I shut my mouth before I said something I didn't think David should know, although something about him seemed so trusting, like I could open up to him no matter what. But like a good girl, I didn't say anything. He frowned at me, wrinkling his nose.

"Who are your friends?" David asked. I thought about telling him, it couldn't hurt, could it? I wouldn't tell him their last names. Not that I knew them anyway.

"Joey," I said simply.

"Anyone else?"

"Well, also Markus."

David scowled.

"Ravens. You look like a Raven."

"You mean the bird?" I asked in surprise, feeling a panic in me start to rise up. "Because I haven't seen any -"

"No, no, no, stupid girl, I mean the people." That caught my attention. I thought almost nobody knew about them.

"How do you know about them?" I asked,

staring at David. I shouldn't have said that, because I was admitting to knowing about them. Stupid me.

"Well, I used to be a Slayer." And like that, I stood at the other end of the table, looking accusingly at David, clearly remembering Joey's warnings about Slayers.

"Whoa, no need to be afraid. I did say *used to be*. I'm not anymore. I left after my wife died in an assassination mission." I relaxed a bit, and sat in a chair across the table from him, keeping distance.

"This food is disgusting. Practically green glop."

I glanced at the very non-green food on his plate. "Yeah or blue glop. Color blind over here."

"True enough. Still gross though."

"Mm-hmm."

"Look, I have to go. My friends are picking me up soon."

The man grabbed a napkin, scribbled on it, then handed it to me.

"If you ever need anything, just call. And keep in mind I know about the Ravens and Slayers and that jazz, so if you need help and can't rely on that Joey person, call."

He grinned at me, and I shoved the paper in my back pocket; I'd throw it away later. Maybe.

I went to the front entrance doors of the hospital to find Joey, Markus, and Sarah already there.

"Finally. You were in there forever. We thought

they caught you after visiting hours and wouldn't let you leave or something," Markus said.

"And thinking that, you didn't come in to find me? Great, glad I can trust you."

He laughed.

"Let's find a taxi. To the compound!" Joey said, raising a fist. We all laughed.

CHAPTER TEN

MARRY

The room Joey sent me to stay in was across from his, and he strictly told me to tell him if I went back into shock or needed anything. He gave me every comfort I wanted. He assigned a Follower to stay with me and get me whatever I wished for; she stocked the fridge full of soda and deserts. I suspected he was trying to distract me from what happened that morning. I hated to admit that he was kinda succeeding.

"Why did the Followers agree to help us?" I asked Kayla. I thought that was her name.

"I'm not sure, ma'am," she whispered.

"Don't call me that. My name is Marry," I said, smiling at her. She blushed.

"I'm sorry," she squeaked. I looked at her. She looked about twelve. At first I was horrified, but she said Followers started working when they were ten, doing small tasks for either the Ravens or Slayers. She said Followers believed children were a lot smarter than humans gave them credit for.

"It's all right; do you want a soda or anything?" I asked her as I opened my fridge. She seemed surprised I asked her.

"I've never had one before," Kayla admitted, blushing when I glanced back at her.

"Do you want to try one?"

"Well... Uh... They're yours... don't you want -"

"I can't drink all of them. It would be a waste. What type do you want?" She stared at me blankly and I realized she probably didn't know any of the types.

"The orange one is good."

"I'll take that then, if you're sure..." I grabbed an orange and a red for me, thrusting the orange in her hands after opening it. She took a tiny taste wearily.

"Do you like it?"

She practically bounced in her chair when she took another drink.

"I love it," she said in between slurps. I smiled. "Thank you," Kayla said.

"How old are you?" I asked. She took another sip then blushed.

"I'm thirteen," she said. "I only have two years until I get to choose. I can't wait."

I looked at her, surprised. "Choose what?"

She looked at me curiously. "Well, choose to continue my training and be a professional and train other Follower kids or get assigned to the Slayers or the Ravens, or train to become a Follower bodyguard to guard other Followers, but usually that's a boring job."

"Which are you going to choose, do you think?"

"I think I want to train other Follower kids. We get another chance to change when we're thirty, but usually we pick for good when we're fifteen. My mom and dad will help advise the first time I pick, and they will agree with what I want to do. But even if they didn't, I am allowed to choose what I want."

"When do you get to use your abilities, if you're always doing things for other people?" As much as I hated drilling info out of her, this was a good chance to learn.

"Well, we get a schedule, mine is Monday, Tuesday, and Wednesday helping people, and all the other days, except Sunday, I train until three thirty p.m." she said, still gulping down her soda. I glanced at the clock. It was nine p.m., crap. She would never fall asleep tonight.

"Are you hungry? I have food in the fridge." Before I got one step toward the fridge, Kayla was standing in front of me, guiding me back into my chair.

"I was told to get things for you, and I can't do that if you keep getting them yourself." Humor sparkled in her eyes as she smiled.

"What do you want?" she said as she opened the fridge.

"A bowl of strawberries, please. And help yourself if you want anything, just not another soda or you'll be up all night buzzing on caffeine." She got me a container of berries and helped herself to a cinnamon apple. I already loved this kid.

"You're great at this. I'm telling Joey about you." I was surprised by how fast she moved. She blushed.

"Thank you, but you don't need to..."

"Nonsense, you're wonderful." She smiled, and I could see she was tired.

"You're exhausted. You should go back to your room and go to bed."

"But Joey told me -"

"Joey doesn't matter. Come on; show me to your room. I'll walk you there."

"You don't need to walk me; I can go on my own." She scowled at me for thinking otherwise.

"You're sure?"

"Yeah. Maybe I'll see you tomorrow around the halls." She left then I closed the door behind her and flopped onto my bed, swiftly falling asleep.

Joey stood next to me, holding me close, screaming at someone I couldn't see to leave. I heard a laugh from the side of the room, and I pressed harder against Joey. He spun around, facing Toby. Tears burned behind my eyes, but I clung to Joey and forced them to stay down.

"Don't hurt her!" Joey growled, holding his sword at ready. The gold hilt gleamed in the dim light.

"Joey, he's my friend! Don't hurt him!" I said to him.

"He won't kill me. If he did, he would die," Toby said. Suddenly Joey jerked away from me as Toby snatched him. He held a dagger at his throat, moving him to the edge of... the world?

"Give yourself to me, Marry, or I will throw him off." Toby said. I was bawling by now, and only managed a moan. He pushed the dagger into his skin, holding him just before the cliff.

"Don't do it, Marry! Run! He'll kill me anyway!" Joey yelled. I tried to lift my feet, but it was like trying to move in syrup. I couldn't think, couldn't move, so I blurted what Joey said not to.

"I'll go! Just don't hurt him," I screamed,

having no conscious control over how loud my voice was. Toby motioned to another guy, and he grabbed me, taking away my staff and binding my hands. Toby smiled.

"You're strong, Marry. You can do it. Use your magic. You have it in you, more than all of us!" Joey said just before Toby pushed him off the cliff.

I woke in a cold sweat, shaking. A glance at the clock confirmed it was the middle of the night. Tears blurred my vision. Stumbling to my feet, I fell into the hall, landing against Joey's door, knocking. I had to check on him, make sure he was still there. Nothing happened for a moment, but then I heard movement.

Joey answered the door, in just pajama pants, his mouth opened as if to say something, but he shut it when he saw me. He gathered me in his arms, guiding me into his room toward the couch.

"What's wrong?" he asked.

"You died; someone threw you off a cliff," I muttered, wanting to curl into a ball.

"It was just a dream," he reassured, placing me on the couch and draping a blanket over me.

"It was so real, though. Toby was there," I told him, as he sat on the couch.

"Just a dream, don't worry. I'm all right." He got up, first making sure I was settled. "Do you want anything? Soda, water, food?"

"Just water." I wiped my eyes, suddenly self-conscious about Joey seeing me like this. He brought back a cup of water and sat next to me on the couch.

"Sorry for waking you up this late," I said. He scowled.

"I told you to come to me if you needed me, plus I don't mind."

"I should probably go back to bed," I said.

"You can sleep on the couch, if you want. It might help with the dreams."

"Are you sure? I don't want to kick you out of your place when I have my own..."

"If you want to sleep here, I don't mind," he said. I blushed, and smiled wearily.

"I think it will help. Thanks," I said. He grabbed an extra blanket and pillow off his bed and put them on the couch for me. I felt guilty, but he didn't seem to mind.

I woke to Joey clanging a wooden spoon on a pan. I opened my sleep-filled eyes and glared at him, rolling over, and placing my pillow over my head.

"Time to get up!" he announced, clanging the metal harder.

"Is this how you treat all your guests?"

"Of course! How else would I treat them?" he asked sarcastically.

"I don't know, maybe wake them gently."

"And how am I supposed to do that when my guest is a very heavy sleeper? I could block off your air, but I thought that'd scare you."

I huffed, and got myself into a sitting position. "I have to go back to my room and get the clothing you bought for me."

"I got it here," Joey said, gesturing to a pile of clothing on the floor. I got up and grabbed the clothing, marching into the bathroom to have a shower and change.

After I got cleaned up, Joey dragged me to the public kitchen to get breakfast. He rummaged through the cupboards, looking for something that met his standards while I ate a bowl of cinnamon oatmeal at a table with several other Ravens. Joey decided on a granola bar and moved next to me, but didn't sit.

"Marry, follow me. We aren't going to sit next to all these sweaty Ravens," Joey said under his breath. I glanced at him to see him turning away. I got up and followed him to a table outside, where only a couple Ravens ate.

"Much better," Joey said, sitting at the table.

"So, are you ready to explain what the hell happened out there?" I asked. We both knew what *out there* meant. I didn't know when I decided I wanted to know, but I did.

"Where should I start?"

"Perhaps the part where I turned into a leopard?" I said, irritated. "Why didn't you tell me I could do that?"

"I told you, Ravens could change form, then I told you that you are a Raven. So essentially, I did tell you."

110

"Whatever," I said. When he didn't say anything else, I gave him a *get on with it* look.

"Well... Your body only changes form when you either really, really want it to change, or when you need to change for survival. I think you changed for survival."

"Ya think, Sherlock?"

"Hey, hey. Don't go all 'that's so obvious you didn't need to point it out' on me. I don't see you knowing how you changed."

"Fine. Continue."

"You might have noticed that you felt very... angry, sad, or happy before you shifted. That's because your brain was being shifted into another form in order to tell your body to change. You could say your brain sort of malfunctioned, giving a false... signal... that an emotion is very high."

"Okay, now on to the man who captured me. Who was he and why did he want to catch me?"

"They call themselves 'The Wreckers.' I have no idea why they choose that name, but they are a group of Followers, Ravens, Slayers, and even humans who are on one of our wanted lists, disagree with how we do things, or hate the fact we use magic. Although the last one usually results in the person going missing. They are essentially a rebel camp we *all* hate."

"Okay, who were those people who helped me, the ones who had electricity coming out of their hands?"

"Those were Slayers," Joey said. I suddenly

had a question I hadn't even thought since I was too relieved that I was rescued.

"How did you know I was captured?" I asked. Joey blushed, I hadn't thought he could.

"Well... Err... I might have sent people to watch you to make sure you -"

"You sent spies to watch me?"

"Only to make sure you didn't get hurt, like you were, and could happen any time -"

"Okay, but how did the Slayers know?"

"We... we don't know."

"Try to touch the magic, reach inside yourself and feel it, embrace it. Like this." Joey reached out his hand palm up. Nothing happened for a few seconds, but then four small balls of water swirling in a circle appeared, hovering above his hand. He had done this a few times now, trying to help me find the magic he said was inside me, although I didn't believe him.

"There are four elements, but each person has the ability to do only one. Mine is water," Joey said. "The air one is interesting, cause you can see a mini tornados swirling in a circle. Cool, right?"

"Yeah, sounds pretty cool. But wait, how can you see air?" I said. Joey shrugged, and I reached my hand out. Closing my eyes, I looked deep inside my brain where I never looked before, deep inside my soul. After at least a minute, I thought I saw, no, felt something. Energy lit up inside me, like it was burning to be used after being locked inside my body for so long. I opened my eyes wide, and stumbled backward from the force of it.

"Did you feel it? The magic?" Joey asked eagerly. I nodded slowly, turning to look at him.

"Try it again, but this time don't let it slip away. Once you have a grasp on it, just will the magic to make a ball of whatever it is above your palm."

"Okay." I closed my eyes and reached out my hand, chasing the magic inside me. Once I got a hold of it, my instincts took over. I had only a small amount of control with my mind. I opened my eyes, and saw all four elements hovering over my hand. My breath caught and I thought I heard a small gasp from Joey.

Quickly, I gained conscious control over these elements. I made them move around, jump over each other, and bounce up my arm. They were like an extra limb. I felt the heat of the flame hovering above my thumb, and the small gust of wind from the visible air above my little finger. Water and soil floated above my palm.

"All four?" Joey asked in disbelief. I wanted to propel the water onto something, and Joey seemed like a nice target. What's the worst it could do? It's just liquid. I focused on the clear substance and made it spring towards him, splashing on his face. I laughed, unable to stop myself.

"Hey. What was that for?" Joey said, also laughing. I continued laughing and focused on getting another water ball to come up. It was much easier to do than last time, but still difficult.

"But really, how did you get all the elements to come up? I have never seen that," he said.

"I don't know. After grasping the magic it was like I wasn't in control anymore. I just did it." I looked around the training room, proud of myself.

I let all the elements disappear, dropping my hand to my side. Joey smiled, looking pleased at the progress we'd made so far.

"I think that's enough for now. You've made lots of progress. Shall we go?" He asked.

"Lets." I replied, following him away.

"Hey, there's Sarah," Joey said.

She looked at both of us and nodded toward me, like she was greeting me.

"Hey, Joey," she said, inclining her head to Joey as well. "What's your progress?"

"It's great. Marry can use all four elements. Isn't that weird?"

"All four?"

"Yep." Joey looked at me. "Marry, you should show her."

"Okay." I focused on the magic and set down my staff. After a second, the elements appeared above my hand. Sarah seemed surprised when they showed up, and just for fun, I made them twirl and fly around. The power felt good to use. Like I was letting go of something inside me after what seemed like decades. Sarah glared at me when she saw Joey's amazed expression.

"Wow," she said. I let the magic fade.

"Did you need something?" Joey asked her.

"No, I just came to tell you they were coming now." She nodded toward the door, where three people stood - they were around my age - with their backs to us. They looked to be training too, and their teacher seemed cruel. They all reached out their left hand, and when the one with blond hair reached out her right hand by accident, it earned her a burn with the fire element on her hand. I focused on the girl who got burnt, studying the back of her head.

With tears in her eyes, the girl turned away from her instructor, rubbing the hand. I got a glimpse of the girl. I knew her.

It was Liz.

Anger swelled inside me toward that instructor, and I turned on Joey. Nobody should be treated that way. Not a soul. It was pretty much child abuse!

"What is he doing to them?" I snapped.

"They are being trained," he said calmly.

"He's torturing them!"

"No, he's teaching them to listen."

"He's hurting them! Aren't you going to do something?"

"Nope. That's how he's supposed to do it." I stared at Joey in disbelief for a long moment. I wasn't letting this fly. Nobody should suffer.

"Fine. I will do something then, if nobody else will."

"No, you're not," Joey said.

"Are you going to stop me?"

"Yes, I would have to."

Without a word, I turned, focusing the magic elements with ease. I barely got a step toward the other trainer when Joey was on top of me, holding my arms firmly in place.

"You can't let him do that to them!" I yelled, struggling with him to let me go. "Let me go!" I yelled.

"I'm afraid I can't do that unless I'm certain you won't try to stop him." A few people nearby watched us, but my mind wouldn't leave the fact those people were physically tortured. I suddenly remembered the elements and gathered the water and earth element balls, mixed them, and flung the mud over Joey's eyes.

It was enough to distract him for a second, which was all I needed. I pulled out of his grasp and ran towards the group. Regaining the water and earth, I figured I'd keep it around in case I needed it later.

I got a good distance before Sarah caught me, but I didn't feel like giving her a facial mud mask. I flared fire where she held me. She probably deserved the fire I pushed into her hands. I continued running then pushed passed the small line of trainees to their teacher, who was in front of one person, about to burn them.

"What do you think you're doing? Disrupting my training," he said, glaring at me.

"That's not how to train, if you ask me. Look at them. They are burned from head to toe." And they were, not here for five minutes and they all had burns up their arms and on their faces.

"This is how we do it. They need to learn to listen to me."

"They can learn without you torturing them!" I was distinctly aware of the dead silence in the training room, and I suspected everyone was looking in my direction.

"Yes, but this is most effective. Also, as you can see, since you're here and disrupting us, you didn't learn to listen to *your* instructors, did you?"

"Oh, I listened, then I made a choice. Unlike you, I haven't been brainwashed to believe everything you guys say, because it's not all right! This is a violation of human rights!"

"You really need to leave now, weakling."

"Don't hurt them!"

"You need to leave NOW."

"Not until you take them to healers and change your style of teaching."

"Don't make me forcefully remove you."

"I'm not moving." He took a deep breath when four fire - balls appeared in front of him. I realized I let my own elements fade.

"Don't make me use fire to make you leave."

"Go ahead. Use your fire. I'm not going anywhere until you take them to healers and stop the torture."

He seemed to sort something else in his head, and then he let it go. Four fire - balls were flung towards me, and my instincts took over. I dodged them effortlessly, and reached inside myself for my own magic, but my anger pushed me to look deeper, listening to my own intuition. I felt another magic and grasped it, letting that part of me take control of my brain again.

My hand rose, palm facing him. I realized four new fire-balls were coming towards me, and failed to dodge all four, one hitting my thigh. I cried out at the pain, but kept my hand raised to him. The pain spurred me into action, and before I could react, a blue blast flew from my hand, hitting him directly in the chest.

He flew back, landing on his back. The place the blast hit was a bit bloody, but wouldn't kill him, I hoped. I walked over to where he lay, limping on my burned leg, and brought up my elements. I heard gasps from the crowd now undoubtedly watching.

"Do you want to feel what your trainees do every time they accidently do something wrong?" I asked. I made the fireball lower next to his arm, then moved it within burning distance. He cried out, and I removed the flame, bringing it back with the others.

"Don't hurt them again. I don't know what I did to you, but I hope there is no permanent damage." I turned to the line of trainees. There, among them, was Liz, her blond hair fell loosely down her back, and her hazel eyes stared at me.

I felt tears brim my eyes at the thought of her here too, and the fact I hurt someone added to my distress. I embraced her in a fierce hug, letting my elements fade. She leaned her head on my shoulder, and I felt a tear hit my neck.

"What did you do to him?" she whispered.

"I don't know, Liz. I don't even know how I did it."

CHAPTER ELEVEN

TOBY

All I saw were Marry's eyes. Their jade green color sparkled in the light, their beauty out of place here. Tears fell onto her cheeks, and I was sure she was the only one who knew why she was crying. Everyone was too stunned to move, or even to talk.

I suddenly feared they would think she was a spy for the Slayers, which she obviously wasn't. I shivered, and instantly recognized the feeling of my Follower being too distracted to keep up my identity as Joey. I had to leave. Marry shouldn't know who I was. No, *couldn't* know. But instead of leaving, I stayed, watching her in her friend's arms, almost hoping she would look up and see who I really was. A long minute passed, and nothing happened, then people started to flee and yell. Marry hadn't lifted her gaze to me yet, but I knew she was going to when two tough-looking Ravens approaching her, looking ready to fight if they needed to.

"Come with us, now," one barked, but the demand didn't have much effect on Marry, she remained, hugging Liz. The two Ravens grabbed Marry and pried her away from Liz, but she didn't bother to fight back, in fact, she looked too tired.

She dragged her eyes from the ground and looked at me. Recognition, shock, and concern crossed her face, and she searched the crowd, probably for Joey. But he was me. Her gaze fell on me, unflinching, and it took a long minute for her to realize I was Joey; she probably saw the color of my eyes, they were identical whether or not I was disguised.

She seemed confused, but then her face darkened in anger. Whether it was because I didn't tell her about this at school or because she figured out I was Joey – it was beyond me.

The men dragged her down the stairs, and the last thing I saw was her long brown hair streaming down her shoulders and back. They were taking her to the White Rooms, but I didn't know if she would stay there without guards absolutely everywhere.

CHAPTER TWELVE

MARRY

Toby was Joey, or Joey was Toby, however it went. I didn't want to believe either, and with no solid evidence, it was easy to convince myself I was wrong. But part of me knew it was true, Toby's Follower used glamor to make him look like Joey, just to keep his identity from me. Why would he hide from me? Did he think I couldn't handle knowing he was Toby?

Maybe he felt bad, and didn't want me to think he betrayed me, not that I thought he did. I was so angry, I wanted to yell at him, to leave this stupid cell, leave this entire Ravens place and go to the Slayers, just to show them all that I could.

But I couldn't. I had no idea where the Slayers were, not to mention getting past all the people who separated me from the school and ground level. It was possible they put me in here, to hold me, until they came to get me out. I settled on the idea that I should wait a while, and if they thought I was too dangerous to let out, then I would start thinking about escaping.

I studied the cell I was in. It was all white with one folding chair in the corner, and a plain metal door. It wasn't going to be easy to escape if I needed to. Of course, what did I expect? A wooden door unlocked and a magical staircase leading to sunlight and rainbows? I sighed out loud, and sat against the wall. All there was to do was wait.

Three hours later though... still nothing.

It was probably well past school hours, but what could I do? It wasn't like my Dad was at home waiting for me, and even if he was, he wouldn't really notice I was late; he would be too busy working. The only thing I could do in this hell-hole was use magic, which got boring and tiring after awhile.

I sat in the small chair and couldn't stop moving, I was so restless. Maybe Toby was really busy, and couldn't get me out. Or maybe he hated me, but I couldn't see it like that.

I heard a creak as the door to the room opened, and I instinctively brought up my elements ready to send them towards the door, since the person could be a potential threat. I looked up and let my elements fade when I saw Toby standing in the doorway, a sad and nervous look on his face. I may be angry at him, but he wouldn't hurt me. I hoped.

"Aren't you going to say something?" he asked.

"What is there to say? That you made me angry? Well obviously." I growled. He looked at his feet, and didn't move from the doorway. "Did you come to take me out of this room?" I asked.

"Can't do that. They think you're a criminal and a spy for the Slayers. But honestly, I don't think they can keep you in here for long."

"So that's it? You're leaving me here to rot?"

"You won't rot. But listen, I have to tell you some things."

"I'll say. Why did you hide from me? That entire Joey thing was a joke. I don't even know why you would try to keep that from me."

"I can be Joey or I can be Toby, but I'm telling you the friendship I feel for you is real, even if my appearance isn't. I didn't want to hurt you, didn't want you to think I was a traitor. I'm not saying I'm not - I'm more of a traitor than you will ever be."

"You have no idea what it is like being me. Everything is against me. Even you."

"I'm not against you. I was trying to make

it easier for you. But I need to tell you something else."

"Go on."

"Well, you know... That rock you saw, the black one at your home, out in the yard, it is actually a... I don't know, a tester I guess. The rock has nothing to do with it really; it just carries the test. When I saw you moved in there, I wanted to make sure you were the descendant of your mother and father.

"To do that, I put the rock there and after I touched the door to the house, everything would get sick on the farm, except anyone or anything who possessed magic. That's why your Dad and Sister are sick but not you, because they aren't magical. There is no other way to find out, unless they bring out their magic themselves."

"You poisoned them? *You're* the one who put their lives in danger then blackmailed me? You said you would heal them if I came and trained, and I have. Get them here and help them!"

"Marry—"

"What? What would you do if you were in my position? Sit quietly and take it? No. You wouldn't, and I won't either. I want my Dad and Sister healed completely!"

"Marry, we can't bring them here. What do you think the doctors will say if we just barge in and say we are taking them? They would never agree."

"Then let me go! I will go to the hospital myself and we can get a Follower to heal them."

"We can't have a Follower doing magic in public! Everyone would see the secret we've hidden so carefully for so long. I can't let that happen."

"Fine. Whatever. Don't let me go then. I will find a way out myself."

"Before I go... There is one more thing I have to tell you."

"Another lie prepared?"

"No... But I have to say... I'm the leader of the Ravens, the top one. Sure, I have advisors and a council, since I'm so young, but still, I'm the one who makes decisions."

"Oh. That much easier to let me out of here."

"It's not that simple. I can't just let you out. But I wish I could."

"You're just a power freak. Always trying to get more power over others."

"No. Actually, I didn't want to be in this position, but after my parents died, I didn't have a choice. You have to understand, everything I said to you, about my personality and about you and anybody else was all true. The only thing I lied about was my identity."

"You probably killed your parents so you could have their position. Doesn't seem too off course even for you." After I said that, I regretted it. His entire face darkened, and grief fell over it. This was obviously a sensitive subject for him.

"I better go," he said, no emotion in his voice whatsoever. "I'll make sure your animals keep getting fed. Bye."

"No - wait. I'm sorry."

"The damage is done. Goodbye, Marry." He turned away but paused before closing the door. "I can't get you out." The door slammed shut behind him.

CHAPTER THIRTEEN

TOBY

I did kill my parents. When they died in that car crash, I was the one driving. I messed up, and hit the other car. I had always thought I killed my parents, because I was the one who caused the crash, but after it happened, people said it was an accident. I never believed them, always knew I killed my parents, but hearing someone else say it, it suddenly felt a lot more real.

Part of me hated Marry for causing me this pain that I wouldn't be feeling if I hadn't gone to her White Room, but the other part of me thinks she didn't know. She didn't know any of this, and it's my fault for not telling her everything in the beginning. I messed up. Just like the car crash.

I sat on the bench in the training room, right where Marry and I sat when we first started training, with my head in my hands, just thinking about everything that had happened and feeling sorry for myself. My parents shouldn't have died from something so mortal. They should have and would have gone down fighting if it weren't for me and my stupidity.

"You okay there, Master Blake?" I looked up, not used to hearing my last name, and was surprised to see Follower Markus leaning over me. I thought he was working at the White-Rooms as a guard. I figured he wanted to be a Raven, but he would never admit it.

"Yeah, I'm fine."

"You don't look fine. What's bothering you?"

"I'm just thinking about the car accident that killed my mother and father."

"What's that got to do with Marry?"

"Marry acted like my mother might have acted, just my mother wouldn't have been as harsh," I lied.

"She's young, my age. She probably didn't know."

"So you don't believe she is a spy?" I asked.

"Not at all. Is it bothering you?"

"No. She is a Slayer or she isn't, either way she's where she needs to be," I said, but I didn't know if I believed it. That was one of the things

I hated about this job - you had to lie so damn often it was irritating.

"Do you think her Mom or Dad will notice she's been gone past school hours? Me and the Followers don't want to deal with the police."

"Her only family here is her father and sister, and they are both in the hospital, remember?"

"Yeah, true."

"Isn't it time for you to give the White Rooms food? You better feed everyone in there." I dismissed him. Not that I didn't like him, I was just not feeling myself and if he stayed any longer I was worried I'd snap.

"Yes, sir!" he said sarcastically as he saluted, and then walked away, flashing a tight lipped grin in my direction.

Chapter Fourteen

Marry

Toby said I had to use pure force of will to get myself into leopard form. He said I had only three types of power I could use, and possibly two more. A knock sounded at the door, and then Markus walked in, carrying a tray of food. I didn't realize how hungry I was until he set it down in front of me and I took a bite. Markus stood watching, amused by my reaction to it.

"You were hungry," he said, smiling.

"I haven't eaten anything in... I don't know... since breakfast." Then it occurred to me that

Markus didn't seem bothered around me like Toby was. "Why aren't you shifting nervously, or eager to leave me here? Even Toby seemed uncomfortable. He said everyone thought I was a spy for the Slayers."

"Everyone does think you're a spy... except me, and possibly Raven Master Blake."

"Can you let me out of this cell?" I asked. Markus studied me for a long second, and then ran a hand over his face.

"Marry, if I could let you out, I would have already. You shouldn't have jumped out at the trainer, but just be good in here and maybe someone will let you out."

Or kill me. The thought pierced my mind, but for some reason I didn't feel as afraid of it as I should have.

"I had to. Couldn't you see? He was torturing people my age, and Liz was with them. I couldn't let them suffer for putting their right hand out instead of left, or having their feet not quite symmetrical. They were being punished for stupid things, and I could do something about it, as much as everyone else could but instead let them be hurt for no reason at all.

"I chose to stand against him instead of sitting in the shadows and watching them be hurt like every other coward in the audience. They deserve punishment more than Liz. You must understand, more than anyone," I said. I wasn't so sure why he would know more than anyone, but looking at his expression, I think he thought I knew something he hadn't told me. Markus stood in silence for a moment, in surprise, perhaps.

"You're right," he said, looking at the ground.

"What?" I said in surprise. I wasn't expecting that.

"You're right. I understand why you did it." He then walked out, shutting the door lightly and locking it behind him without another glance in my direction.

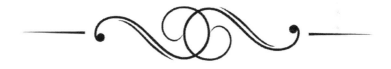

I woke with Markus leaning over me, yanking my hands behind my back and putting them in handcuffs.

"Hey, what's this about?" I muttered as I was pulled up to stand. Then I saw Sarah and Toby by the entrance to my White-Room, just watching. Sarah grinned, and I glared at her.

"This wasn't my choice," Markus whispered to me when Sarah wasn't looking. I shot a confused glance at her and Toby. Only Markus acknowledged me. I wouldn't blame Markus; no, I'd blame Sarah. Toby seemed uncomfortable and wouldn't make eye contact.

"Hey, Marry. I'm speaking on Commander Toby's behalf, since apparently he can't, for some reason," Sarah snickered. "So, your little spectacle yesterday was very unexpected to say the least, but thank the gods we got you under control so quickly." I clenched my fists. She smiled, obviously trying to make me angry.

"The problem is we can't find any evidence of you being a spy. It seems you've already got one or two people who believe you aren't. I don't believe it for one second. That you aren't a spy, that is." Something about her statement bothered me. "Perhaps you're an assassin. Your very... unique relationship with Toby *and* Markus could be for show, trying to get close to them and ... "

"Stop blabbering and get on with it *Now*," Markus said in a dangerous voice that rung with authority, though I doubted he had any over her. She glared at him. Markus still stood behind me, holding my wrists tightly.

"All right. So, we weren't sure what to do with you, and we can't possibly leave you here to think about an escape plan when so much stuff needs finishing, so I decided you are going to help out in the research labs."

"We actually know everything that's going to be tested on you. It won't kill you; but it'll more than likely hurt. I was at the meeting," Markus whispered in my ear. Sarah saw and glared daggers. I was still frozen in anger and fear that Sarah would arrange that. I would *not* be a test subject willingly, not that I'd done all that much willingly anyway. Markus guided me out of the cell, following Toby and Sarah down a hallway.

He stopped at a glass door, and I could see the disapproval on Sarah's face. She was obviously eager to get going.

"You're strong," Markus said, quickly opening the glass doors and striding through, tugging me along with him. People researching one thing or another hunched over books and computers, scribbling rapidly in thick notebooks. There were multiple glass-walled rooms with people inside injecting themselves, and others outside studying the results. None of them even glanced up as we entered.

"Go fetch Dr. Dobson. I'll watch her," Sarah said, glancing at me. Markus obeyed, leaving for less than a minute before coming back with a short man at his side. I looked at Mr. Dobson. His wrinkled face and bald spot made him look pretty old. I would have guessed he was well over sixty.

"Ah, hello, Dr. Dobson. Do you have the tests ready?" Sarah asked.

"Oh, yes. Everything is prepared for our guest. Thank you again for coming, Miss Clad. It really is a help."

Like I had a choice I thought, but I was grateful he thanked me. That went a lot farther than it probably should have.

"Come along, my dear." He scurried toward the corner. Sarah dragged me along, but Markus kept a close eye on us, hovering nearby. When we got there, Sarah took out a key and released my hands from the shackles. I rubbed my wrists;

they were slightly red where the metal scraped my skin.

The man grabbed a liquid vial from his desk, putting it in a slot to the glass room closest to us. Then he grabbed a syringe and approached me.

"This is just so we can read your reaction to the tests," he said as he injected me, then he opened the door to the room.

"Okay, dear, just walk in and sit on the bench. The gas shouldn't hurt you, but it might, so be prepared." Dr. Dobson said. Sarah pushed me in, closing the door behind me. In the far edge of the enclosure there was a white bench that didn't have a back, and I took a seat on it.

Nothing happened at first, but then Dr. Dobson pressed a button and a faint blue fog blew into the room. My mind at first told me not to breath it in, but then I remembered Markus's words. As soon as I inhaled, I'd probably choke or something, and I braced myself, but nothing happened.

Sarah looked annoyed at my reaction after the fog dissipated, and even Markus had a scowl of confusion on his face, though he looked relieved. Through the glass I heard one murmur "why" and "of worked," but I couldn't hear all of it. Dr. Dobson gave me thumbs up, and walked into the room with a syringe.

"Ah, that's a girl. You were fantastic! There is one more to do before I'll show you the results. Every couple of tests and I'll show you, sound good?" he asked. I kind of liked him, despite everything, so I nodded. "Will you lay down for me? It makes the injection get to the target area faster, in this case."

"Sure," I said, laying back on the bench.

"On the count of three, I will inject you. One... Two." The needle popped through my skin and he rushed back to his computer, closing the door behind him. I felt fine for a while, but then it hit me. The piercing pain was so intense and so unexpected that I was beyond screaming.

My back rose off the bench, and tears streamed down my face. All I could hold on to were Markus's words, so I repeated them over and over again in a sad attempt to block the pain. As I went numb, the poison he injected into me faded enough for me to get feeling again, then came back in full force.

Sarah was going to pay for this. I doubted she even knew how bad this hurt, and I didn't think it was possible to explain it. It wasn't even imaginable. I clung to Markus's advice trying to remain conscious as I waited for the poison to wear off.

It seemed like years later when Markus rushed into the room with a syringe and plunged it into my arm. For a moment Markus, held my hand as I writhed in pain, and I wondered what in the world he was doing. I thought he wasn't allowed to be in here. I started to feel better until the pain was just a dull throb, and I found myself curled against Markus, shivering, but taking comfort in his presence.

I peeked at Sarah, and saw her staring at us with a look of disgust. She'd probably never done anything nice for anything or anybody. Markus whispered reassuring things into my ear until Dr. Dobson strode in with another syringe, but Markus carefully got up and intercepted him.

"You can't inject her with that. By the sounds she made from the last one, it seemed like she was being killed," Markus growled.

"I must test these on someone, Follower Markus," he said, glaring at him, trying to go around Markus. He just stepped in the way again.

"You will *not* inject her with anything else," he said firmly, challenging.

"Yes, I will. Sarah said for me to inject her with this." He held up the syringe. "Don't worry. It shouldn't hurt her like the last one." I saw from the corner of my eye Sarah coming into the room, but Markus didn't notice.

"Get away from her. She's not having another syringe embedded into her today or else I will embed that into *you*," Markus said. Dr. Dobson tried yet again to step around Markus, but failed when Markus was faster. "No."

"Markus!" But I was too late. Sarah hit his head in one quick strike, hard enough for him to go down. He didn't fall unconscious, but he didn't get up, either. Dr. Dobson looked at my protector with minor concern, but Sarah glared at him on the floor, then grabbed Dr. Dobson's syringe and plunged it into Markus. Markus screamed, and the sound sliced through me like cutting a cake.

A sudden need to defend and protect Markus like he did for me surged, taking over the small part of my mind uninjured from the previous test. How could she hurt him so bluntly, without even seeming concerned? I couldn't believe her. I knew she was annoying, and mean at times, but this?

I didn't think she'd go this far, even for her. When Sarah moved toward him again, I found myself on my feet in front of her so fast that the world blurred a spilt second before I was there. She smiled down at me, looking unamused, even slightly irritated.

"When Markus didn't help you out of the White-Rooms, I thought he might actually be more worthy than I first saw him to be. What a shame it is that he turned on us." She sneered.

Rage pumped through my blood, and all I could do was cower behind my arms and scrunch my eyes closed as electricity shot out of every part of my body, driven by the need to keep Markus safe. The glass room shattered into millions of pieces when the electricity hit it, and Sarah fell to the ground. I gasped in horror, staring down at myself.

Sarah got up and stalked towards me, throwing a punch in my direction. My hand grabbed her fist midair and twisted until I heard a sickening crunch. I barely felt the effort, but I couldn't tell if that was because my brain didn't register it or because it actually wasn't an effort.

That energy flowing through me, I felt a connection to it and knew that if I managed to summon it consciously, I could use it again with minor effort. Sarah scooted away, cradling her arm to her body, and I fell back in horror, the need to defend Markus gone in an instant. How could I let myself do that? Nobody deserved to have their arm broken on purpose... Did they?

I couldn't bear to look at Sarah. Cruel or not, she didn't deserve that. She was letting Dr. Dobson feed me poisons, but did that justify such harsh punishment? No, I reassured myself, but she shouldn't have made me endure such testing, either. I sat on the bench, stunned out of my senses, staring into my lap without seeing it. I hardly heard or felt guards dragging me back to my White-Room—nor did I really care.

How did I manage to get that much electricity out of me? When I saw those Slayers fighting, they only had one or two beams each, and it was coming out of their hands. Maybe every Slayer could do what I just did, and could move just as fast.

There must be others like me out of the billions on earth. Someone else must feel the bizarre things I feel, have the talents I have, but still barely had a claim over them. I couldn't be the only one like this. It had to be impossible... But maybe it wasn't. Maybe there weren't others.

Maybe I really was alone.

"Why did you do it?" a random what-I-thought-was-suppose-to-be interrogator asked me. She'd asked me this same question about twenty times, and each time I told her the same thing. After time to calm and think about what happened, I realized my actions against Sarah were perfectly valid, and I was actually helping more people by hurting her than not. So I stood by my choices, because I wasn't backing down anymore, and I wasn't going to regret everything I did, even if it was something I would have thought was awful in the past.

"I didn't have a choice. It was like a caged animal inside me, and when I opened the cage gate it wanted *out*, and I didn't have any say in that matter," I said for the billionth time. "And when a malicious intent attacked its comrades, it came to their defense."

"I'm assuming the caged animal is you, the 'comrades' are Markus, and the wild animal is Sarah?"

"I suppose."

"So you got mad at Sarah because you thought she was behind the misunderstanding with the fluid testing."

"I suppose."

"What do you think your punishment should be?"

"When do I get to leave your office and go back to my White Room?"

"After you answer my questions."

"I am answering your questions."

"Not to my approval,"

"Does your approval matter?"

"Don't say such disrespectful things." It went like that for a long while, but she never failed to bring it back to the same question over and over and over again, and I never failed to answer it.

CHAPTER FIFTEEN

TOBY

"How the hell did she do it?" I asked Lorene, the interrogator. "I don't know, sir," she replied. This was really getting annoying; she was an interrogator, she should know these things. It was her *job* to know.

"Well, figure it out! Why do you think she did it? Was it because of Markus or Sarah?" When she didn't answer, I went on, "You must at least have an answer to that?"

"Well, she did say one thing about why, sir."

"Spit it out."

"She made a comparison of her, Sarah, and Markus. She said she let a caged animal out, then the animal's comrades were attacked, and it went to their defense," she said. "We later determined that Marry was the caged animal, Markus was the comrades, and Sarah was the threat, sir."

"So she was protecting Markus from Sarah?" As this was going, I knew I was going to have to go see Marry for myself.

"That's what it looks like, sir."

"What was Sarah doing to Markus?"

"We're not sure yet."

"Should I ask Marry myself?"

"If you wish, but she *is* dangerous, sir."

"Nonsense. Where is she?" I said. Saying things like "nonsense" was another of my sad attempts at trying to act older and mature enough for my rank here; which I wasn't, but nobody let me pass it on to someone else, saying it's "in my blood" to lead.

"I sent her back to her White-Room."

"Grab me a coat. Also, fetch a couple helper Followers to ready Marry's old room here. And set up security cameras and people to watch them."

I reached Marry's White Room, and stood in front of the door. I kept questioning myself. Should I talk to Marry again? Would she still act as nice as she used to around me? I wasn't sure. The thing was I really didn't have any say in letting her out. This is the least I could do; I reassured myself as I opened the door and looked inside.

Marry wasn't there.

Chapter Sixteen

Marry

"**D**AVID!" I exclaimed into the phone. "As soon as you get this message, CALL ME." Markus huffed in amusement at the tone of my voice.

"We're fine. Everyone who looks at us will see some random Followers. They'll probably think we're dating or something," he said, giving me a thumbs up. I almost laughed. Almost. I called David again but he didn't answer, so I left another message.

We got to Markus's room without incident,

and I instantly started ranting about how David wasn't answering.

"Maybe he's asleep," Markus offered.

"To hell he's asleep."

"Just saying, he might be." Markus shrugged.

"They're gonna notice I'm gone any minute."

We sat in silence for a second, but the buzzing of Markus's phone caused me to jump up. Looking at the caller ID, I was pleased to see David calling back.

"What's up, man?" David asked when I held the phone to my ear.

"Uh, David, it's Marry."

"Ohhh, hi, Marry."

"You need to come pick us up."

"Whoa, whoa, whoa. Why?"

"No time to explain. Be at the school in twenty."

"What school—"

"Winderly High. The one that the Ravens are housed under." I said, and then hung up. Markus looked at me.

"You do know nobody has ever escaped our White-Rooms alive, right?"

"We haven't escaped yet, so we can't say we are the first," I said. "You ready to go?"

"Yep, disguise is up." We left his room. Followers and Raven guards jogged past us in small groups as we worked our way through the building, and when I saw Toby at the end of a hall coming our way I nearly froze in fear. Markus touched my arm, urging me on. Toby was accompanied by at least three Followers and Sarah, all of which seemed to be guarding him. He was talking to someone, in an urgent tone. As we came closer I heard some of his conversation.

"—she must have taken him," Toby said.

"Maybe he went willingly. Did you guys see him do anything suspicious before this?" Sarah asked the Followers. They all mumbled a 'no'.

"It's entirely possible Marry took him. But that doesn't make a lot of sense, cause they seemed friends."

"Possible," the girl Follower agreed.

"Unless he decided to pull another of his crazy leave-for-vacation-without-warning-for-two-weeks' stunts. And at the same time as Marry's disappearance," Toby said. They were talking about Markus. I instantly regretted asking him to come. I probably ruined his life here at the Raven compound. I didn't know about his family, but if they worked here... he'd probably never see them again. Toby glanced at us.

"Hey, you two, with me." Markus did a small salute, but I was frozen in a big puddle of fear. Markus pushed me lightly ahead of him, and I stumbled to catch up to Toby, staying at least a few steps behind him. After a few minutes of walking, Toby pointed to a random door that didn't look at all significant.

"Guard this. Let no one in," he said. Markus and I stood by the door, and when he rounded a corner, we instantly raced in the other direction.

"That was close," I muttered under my breath to him.

"Not really. We had it completely under control. We only would have been screwed if he gave us each different jobs."

It didn't take us long before we got to the stairs and happily climbed. About three steps up, a buzzing sound echoed through the stairwell, then a lady's voice projected fairly quietly throughout the hall. I was suddenly struck that all this disruption was because of me. I guess they didn't get a lot of action around here.

"We need thirty Ravens to get outside of the school and patrol the surroundings. Don't upset the humans, and *don't* attract attention. Meet at the lounge. Don't let anyone in or out of the area unless it's a human. I repeat, we need thirty Ravens to get outside of the school and patrol the surroundings. Master Blake's orders." The microphone went dead.

"Damn," I said under my breath.

"We gotta hurry. Like, super-fast so we can get out before they do. I've seen them do this kind of thing once or twice, and they'll be out there and organized in, maybe, 5 minutes at the longest." Five minutes. We needed to *hurry*. I skip two and three steps, flying up the stairs at top speed. Markus caught up to me easily.

When we got on the basement level of the school, there were only a few Ravens around and we avoided them easily.

"All right, I see the exit to the first level of the school, when we're climbing the stairs, don't look back. People will suspect something if you do. Act like you have a purpose," Markus said. He led us to the stairwell and started pulling me up. I couldn't help it - I looked back, and I made eye contact with a Raven. I turned away and bolted up the stairs.

When we reached the school level, we ran towards the exit. We had about three minutes, maybe less if Markus was right about the timing. A few Ravens looked at us on our way, but lots of people were hurrying around to do their own jobs. We weren't an abnormality, but maybe in five minutes? Everyone would probably be settled down if they were as organized as Markus said.

When we got to the front doors, Markus shoved it open and I ran through, him behind me.

"Did anyone see you on the basement level?" Markus asked.

"I'm not sure," I said, too petrified to tell him when I looked down the hall, I did see some-one, and they saw me, too. I wanted to tell him I heard Toby calling people underground, right now. Somehow, I could hear through the ground and the ceiling. But my lips were sealed shut, only letting lies flow beyond my command of better judgment. I struggled to gain control of my body, and I could barely tell if it was my fear not letting me say the right thing or something else.

"Let's go. Quickly," I managed.

"Is David here yet?" he asked.

"We better check."

Markus led the way, setting a brisk pace toward the front of the school. I pushed him forward, eager to go before they got to us. We finally reached the sidewalk and looked around. There wasn't a car in sight.

"Where is he?" I exclaimed, suddenly frantic. I punched his number on my phone and waited.

"Hi, Marry. Sorry for the hold up. There's a bit of traffic y'see." he said as soon as he picked up.

"You're not here!" I exclaimed.

"No, I'm not there yet. As I said, there's traffic. It's rush hour." he said.

"Damn it, David! You need to come *extremely* quickly, it's very important."

"Okay, okay, I'm coming. See you in a couple minutes. Maybe this traffic will clear out." He then hung up. I thought I saw flickers of people hovering around in the more shadowy areas around the school, but I might have imagined them. Markus glanced at me.

"Marry, stay calm, but I think we have a tail. Get a stick like the staff you first practiced with," he said under his breath, gesturing to a tree nearby. I practically tripped over my feet when looking. I found a short, but sturdy one. When I got back, Markus had his pocketknife in hand.

"Okay, Marry, they will attack any moment. There are probably a lot of Followers here to make the scene look different for the humans, but things will still happen. You need to stay behind me at all times," he said calmly, though his eyes darted frantically. "They only want me. They'll probably just subdue you if they know who you are, so I'm going to drop the disguise. You *can't* be afraid of them. Fight back."

"Markus - I can't - I can't kill someone - I just can't - I'm sorry."

"You don't need to kill them, but they might surround me and I can only take on a few. I will *need* help. Use your magic."

"I don't know how."

"Just try. Knock people out if you need to. But remember: they are your *enemies*."

"Markus?"

"Yeah?"

"Try not to hurt people too badly. Please," I pleaded. He seemed pained.

"I need to. They will *kill -*"

"I know. But don't hurt them if they don't need to be hurt. Please, Markus," I said. "Promise me you won't on purpose." He looked at me.

"I'll try," he said. A minute or so later, I saw another flicker of a person from the shadows, and I cringed back. My palms were sweaty and my knuckles white from gripping the stick. I wished David was here to -

"Now!" I heard someone yell, and we were suddenly surrounded by about eleven people with swords and knives, and behind them I saw five Followers in a circle with their eyes closed, concentrating.

Markus was in action in a matter of milliseconds, but I was legitimately glued to the ground in my own fear. Things happened in a flash, and Markus was thrashing against seven people with his small knife while the rest were holding my arms and legs and I was helpless and I was going to die and I was paralyzed and suddenly they were all on the ground while I was still screaming at them to stop.

The world blurred around me, and the last thing I saw was Markus's astonished face staring at me in bewilderment and concern.

CHAPTER SEVENTEEN

TOBY

"How in all the hells did you let her get away?" I practically yelled at the guards. I was outraged they would let her escape, because they must have. Nobody had ever gotten out of our White-Rooms unless we let them out. There was no way she was an exception.

"Sir - we didn't - we have no idea how she got out. We were in these exact corridors when she walked into her White-Room with an escort. The only strange thing that happened was John was knocked out somehow. He doesn't remember anything."

"Why didn't you tell me that earlier? That opens a million situations for me alone. Where was he posted?" Oh, my god, why didn't he tell me this sooner? She could have done thousands of things to make that happen, and it might've even helped me find where she was hiding.

"Over here, sir," the guard said quietly, hurrying through the halls toward wherever he was stationed as guard. I was almost certain someone let her out of here. I just had to figure out who. The guard finally stopped near the staircase leading to the floor where the sleeping quarters were.

"He was stationed here, sir," he said, motioning near the staircase.

"Did anything else happen? Did Markus take her food or water; take her for the once a day walk, or anything else?"

"Well, sir, she did go to the bathroom, and none of us saw her return. We assumed Markus took her for the walk afterward, and that was about thirty minutes before her escape."

Why couldn't people just tell me these things right away? It took him ten minutes just to tell me about the guard, and those ten minutes could be Marry getting away.

"Can you not just tell me everything that happened without me asking specifically?" I said. The one person I *wanted* to keep in the White-Rooms escaped, possibly because of Sarah's stupid idea to take her to the experimental room.

And she blamed me too, Sarah saying she was speaking on *my* behalf, which was a lie. Markus must have helped her escape, I realized. He probably disguised themselves as two random Followers and walked out of here peacefully. That girl I saw walking through the hall with another Follower seemed to have tensed when I got close. What if she was Marry and Markus in disguise? I'd better send someone to make sure they're still guarding the camera room. Extra precaution was always good.

"Send someone to check the monitoring room. Make sure there is one female and one male Follower guarding it. Tell me if they're there or not."

"Yes, sir." He scurried away.

CHAPTER EIGHTEEN

MARRY

A blurry figure appeared in front of me and I heard noise, though I couldn't translate anything into words. All I could think was how so completely *exhausted* I was. Fatigue dragged at my limbs and pulled at my mind, beckoning for rest and sleep. I battled it, trying to stay awake long enough to talk, to find the energy to move my lips into sentences, trying desperately to bring my eyes into focus, though it was only moments before it was useless and I was pulled back into the bliss of sleep.

Hours later, the fluorescent light beamed . . .

The fluorescent light beamed through my closed eyes, and I wondered how in the world I ever managed sleep in this harsh environment. Rolling onto my back, I cracked my sleep-shut eyes open and was momentarily blinded.

"How are you feeling?" Markus asked. I jumped, turning to see he was sitting next to me.

"I don't know," I replied, squeezing my eyes shut.

"You must have regained your energy if you can talk."

"Where are we?" I asked. I didn't recall anything really. The last thing I remembered was everyone collapsing unconscious. He looked down.

"We're at the Slayers' place. They gladly accepted you, and didn't mind in the least me coming along." I jolted up in my bed, and Markus pushed me down. "Slowly," he said.

"What? We're at the Slayers' compound? How'd we get here? How long was I out?" I asked, getting up almost too fast to be considered slow. Markus glanced down. "How long was I out?" I asked again.

"Four days," he said. Four days? How did I sleep that long? As I started to remember the details of what happened, I snapped up.

"Are the people okay - none of them died, right? Please, please, please tell me they are all right," I pleaded. Markus looked down, then to the side, then to the other side. Finally he looked at me.

"A few died. Most of them were only unconscious though."

I dropped my chin to my chest for a second and prayed they made it safely to heaven. Since I wasn't religious, I didn't know any fancy things to say to acknowledge their deaths, heck, I didn't even know the people, but I felt it was necessary to at least recognize them.

"Why are we here?" I asked urgently.

"We didn't really have anywhere else to go. The Ravens saw David's car and were following us. The only place we would be safe was with the Slayers, and it was simple since they were, on a purely technical level, helping us get away."

"Okay, so what happened, like, with *me*? Why have I been unconscious all this time? I remember what happened, but how did I do it and what did I even do?"

"When Slayers use their electricity, it always comes out of a part of their body. They think you somehow projected electricity into the part of the Ravens' minds that controls their consciousness and zapped it, making them pass out. The Slayers can't make the electricity start from somewhere other than their own body, so the fact you could start it *inside* someone's brain other than your own was amazing for them. They think you're a god."

"Is that what I did? Do the Slayers think it will make any permanent damage? Why did I go unconscious for so long then?" I asked. I could have hurt them badly. I prayed silently to any god that was listening that they were all right.

"No, the Slayers are pretty sure you contained it only in the smallest part of their brain, only causing them to faint. The reason you probably fell asleep for so long was mostly because you fainted for about a day, and since you have barely used your power at all in your lifetime it surprised your body so much that when you grabbed hold of that much power it overloaded. It will never happen again for the same reason now that your body is semi familiar with that power."

"Oh."

"I'd better tell someone you're awake. As I said, they think you're a god and are eager to meet you. Get dressed; there are clothes in your armoire," he said, gesturing to the behemoth piece of furniture in the corner of the room. "I'll see you later," he said, patting my shoulder as he walked out of the room, closing the door behind him.

The room was a light blue and white, with only the bed I was in, a fridge, a few upholstered chairs and small table along with the armoire. My gaze landed on the fridge, and my stomach growled - I was starving. Pushing the tangled blankets off, I walked over to the mini-fridge, helping myself to a juice box. I put the empty container on top of the fridge, then made my way to the armoire and looked inside.

I was overwhelmed by clothing.

Colors exploded around me, bursting to be seen. Tight dresses and flowing robes crammed together, beckoning to be worn. Bright greens, blues, and any other color you could imagine were mixed into clothing, and when I opened the rack to look at a particular dress, I saw another layer behind them. I had to admit, I hated dresses. The way dresses sat on my hips and teased my legs bugged me, but these dresses seemed worth it. They just looked so *beautiful*.

Checking below them, I saw shoes of all different types. High heels, flats, runners, boots, everything. Next to them were socks. They were, well, your average socks. Nothing special. I looked at the dresses, contemplating which one I should wear. Pushing the dresses out of the way, I observed that in the back layer there were sweatpants and T-shirts. This would be one of the only times I'd say it, but I think I'd rather wear one of the cool dresses. They were so *gorgeous*. Grant would have loved this... I wished she was here.

A shiny red dress caught my eye, and I pulled it out. It had sleeves that went to the elbow, and the end folded on itself. The red was only faintly shiny with small flecks of gold littered throughout. I felt the inside and was surprised when I felt it was soft, compared to other dresses. Taking it out, I decided I would try it on.

A couple minutes later I was tucked into the dress, and it was the most comfortable thing I had ever worn. The fabric broke from tight to skirt just above my belly-button, and stopped at my thighs. I examined myself in the mirror. The dress fit perfectly, and my wavy brown hair -that was in knots- looked good with the red. I looked really good, for me.

Going back to the armoire and digging through it, I found a pair of boots fairly high with red lining and laces, and holy *crap*, it matched the dress perfectly. I decided not to put them on until Markus got here to get me, so I put them by the door and went into the bathroom. The counter was filled with cosmetics, but I ignored all of it, grabbing the hairbrush and yanking it through my clean but knotted hair. I was halfway done when I heard Markus come in and say my name.

"One second!" I yelled, brushing through a couple more times. He yelled again, and I did one last brush and opened the door, walking into the main room. Markus stood near the door, eating potato chips. He blinked at me, and it was a couple seconds until he spoke,

"You look nice," he said. I blushed.

"Thanks," I said. "Are the Slayers ready for me?"

"Yeah, they're ready."

I put my boots on, testing the comfort. They were not very comfortable, but it made up for the perfectness of the dress. I followed Markus down the hall nervously. What if they attacked me for being a Raven? No, they would have killed me when I was asleep. What if they wanted to take info from me? So many if's, but Markus was right when he said we didn't really have anywhere else to go, and if he didn't think they'd hurt me, I trusted him.

The front of my dress tickled my legs, and I smoothed it out. Markus stopped in front of a door and looked at me sideways. "They're very formal so don't try to make jokes or laugh. I learned that the hard way." He knocked on the door. A second later a man a bit shorter than me opened the door and his whole face lit up.

"Come in, come in, young magician. We've been waiting for you," he said excitedly as he held open the door. I walked in nervously. He wore a white suit with black gloves, tie, and shoes, and I was relieved I didn't dress overly formal, even if I picked one of the less formal dresses. His hair was down to his ears, and jet black. "Sit, we shall talk. Help yourself to the cookies and sandwiches. You must be hungry." He motioned toward a couch, then a side table with food. I ate so much in such a short time it was embarrassing, but he didn't comment. Markus and I sat and Shorty sat across from us. He seemed so ecstatic and happy, and I had no idea why.

"Oh, I'm so, so sorry. I forgot my manners in my excitement! My name is Vayne Zahavi. I'm the monarch of the Slayers; they are so excited to meet you." Markus said they thought I was a god because I did something with the electricity to make the Ravens unconscious, but I didn't expect someone like Vayne to be so joyful.

"Why are you guys so accepting of me? I was

from the Ravens. We both were," I said. Markus shot me a look I couldn't quite place.

"Well, my dear, we have been waiting for you to come along for centuries! The holy majestic god told us you would come. They say you will make peace with us and the Ravens - help the world believe and know about our presence, and use our powers for a greater good!

"We have waited for you to rise and approach us for years, and we wouldn't let down the opportunity to bring you here for anything." The holy god told them about me? What holy god? And I never really "rose up and approached them." It was more like a this-or-death kind of thing.

So many questions buzzed in my head, but as I opened my mouth to voice one of them, Vayne continued. "Now, my magician, you simply must tell me everything that happened that evening when the Ravens were attacking you when you did that marvelous work of art!" he said, staring at me.

I didn't know what to say. I didn't really know what happened that evening, so how was I supposed to answer? I settled on telling him the whole story, everything that happened, and hoped to their holy god he was talking about that. He was a nice man and wasn't going to manipulate me. He looked at me a moment after my story.

"My goodness! I never thought someone could have such an extraordinarily high amount of power! Simply amazing, is what that is. You are most definitely sent by the heavens as a message," he said.

I honestly, truly, thought he was a nice man, but when he said things like that? How does one even respond? Should I laugh? Was he joking? Should I bow my head or smile or frown or what? "I know this must be so much for you to take in, and with you just waking it doesn't help either, but you really must understand how badly the other Slayers want to meet you." He said, "I cannot keep them waiting forever!"

I absolutely did *not* want to meet any more Slayers, not because they were bad people, but because I needed to rest. I felt fatigue drag at my limbs a little more every minute and I really wanted to eat and relax. "Maybe later today will work. I can bring them into the main group meeting place," he said. I tried to smile, to act normal.

"No, you can't keep them waiting forever. But Vayne, I'm quite tired and hungry, and I also want to learn how this place works first. And if you don't mind me asking, I'd like to meet them in a maybe a couple days. I really hope this doesn't offend you, but I really need some time to settle in." He seemed confused for a minute but then he seemed to understand what I was asking.

"Oh yes, of course. What on planet Earth was I thinking? You definitely need time to settle in. Yes, yes, I understand."

"We'll get going then, unless you have anything else to say?" Markus said. Vayne looked at me.

"All Slayers must be in their rooms by nine p.m., and asleep with their lights off at ten. Everyone must wake by eight thirty, and be getting breakfast by ten a.m. Except on Sundays, in which case we go to sleep at nine and wake up at nine thirty, and you can get breakfast any time before eleven." They had strict rules around here.

The Ravens seemed more laid back, but the Slayers must've felt it necessary to have it strict. Toby did say once they had a bedtime. I'd thought he was joking. "You two can have breakfast with me in exactly three days; we'll visit the Slayers right after. Put on a nice dress and get your hair done. I'll send someone to help you that morning." I nodded, following Markus as he stood.

"Farewell, magician. We are so flattered to have you as a guest," he said as Markus and I left the room. I immediately turned to him.

"Where is David?" I asked in alarm. I only met him once, but I thought he was pretty cool for an old man. I dearly hoped nothing happened to him.

"Oh, he's a retired Slayer or something. They gave him a room beside yours."

"Oh," I said. We walked on down the hall for a few seconds. "Wait, where are *you* staying?" I asked, realizing they might not have welcomed him like they welcomed me or David. I swear Markus blushed.

"Well... Umm... I'm actually staying in your

room," he said. "On the couch," he added hastily. I nodded.

"Wanna train for a bit? I could show you how to use a staff better, and we still have a couple hours to kill before we have to sleep."

"No," I replied. I really did *not* want to go train. The exhaustion wasn't completely erased, and people were probably going to be there, and I didn't feel like being close to anybody other than Markus or David.

He looked at me seriously. "You honestly have to learn sometime. You remember what happened four days ago? That could happen again at *any* time and I don't want you to be defenseless and only able to use magic," Markus said, and then added. "Actually, it's not a choice. I will drag you to the training room if I have to. *Please*, don't make me do that."

"Fine," I grumbled. "I have to stop at my bedroom so I can change. But *don't* expect me to hurt you or anyone else while practicing. I've hurt enough people for one... four days, I guess."

CHAPTER NINETEEN

MARRY

I pulled one eye open through sheer force of will, and saw Markus staring at me. I groaned, rolling over and pulling the pillow over my head. "C'mon, sleepy head. We're gonna practice your magic today with David," Markus chorused. Since I had met with Vayne, every spare moment had been constant running and training, so in other words, it had been constant torture as far as I was concerned.

My days consisted of being woken by Markus, getting breakfast, running the track, and then training. Ate lunch, then trained. Dinner at five, then train until passing out on my bed at nine.

After I dressed, Markus dragged me to the really cool indoor track I'd come to dread. We ran five laps, no stopping allowed, and while he was always laughing from the joy of it, I could hardly keep myself upright after we were done. Panting, I quickened my speed to catch up to Markus.

"How do," I paused to take in a gulp of air, "you keep going?"

"Practice, mostly. I've run on tracks similar to these just short of every day in the last couple years." He slowed to match my pace. "Maybe after you greet the Slayers we can increase to ten laps."

I grimaced, already imagining the torture that would put me through.

"Now, shush and just run," he said.

I tried so hard not to puke up my innards after we finished running, but it was no use. Vomiting over the garbage bin, I decided I should skip breakfast. It wasn't like I could ever keep it down anyway. Markus led me to the training room attached to the track, and David, thank the gods, wasn't there quite yet, so I sat for a while to catch my breath.

"You're getting better at running. When we first started you gagged longer and slowed down faster," Markus said. I glared at him, suddenly angry at myself for not even knowing how to run.

"I don't think that has *anything* to do with me

getting better," I said. Markus just smiled, waving to David as he entered the room.

Training for hours was horrible, as it always was. I couldn't do anything David demonstrated or even summon any magic. When I used it in that laboratory at the Raven place, I felt so sure I could use it again, but it seemed that wasn't the case. David and Markus seemed unconcerned, and said I'd get it eventually, but when I looked closely at Markus, I knew something was bugging him.

After negotiating some down time, I sat on the sofa in some lounge-type place. I reached for the coffee table where magazines sat, flipped through them, relaxing my brain. I wished I knew where the library was in this place, if there was one, because real books would be much better than magazines.

A couple minutes later a person entering the room pulled my attention, and I looked up. The man staring back at me looked like he was around thirty, and he seemed pleased to see me. He wore a formal suit that resembled a uniform, so when he sat on another pristine couch in the lounge, he fit in quite well.

"Hi, Marry. I'm an adviser for the royal family and Mr. Zahavi. It must be very difficult for you to understand our ways and why we do things, so Mr. Zahavi sent me to help you and Markus out a bit," he said, a smile tugging at the edges of his lips.

It was true - I definitely didn't know anything about the Slayers, or Ravens, yet really; only the bare bone basics. His voice softened and went significantly quieter. "Mr. Zahavi plans on attacking the Ravens in a couple weeks, and he hopes to end this war once and for all. The gods told us we need you to win, that you are the key to our survival, and now that we have you, Mr. Zahavi sees no reason to wait. He does know, however, it may be difficult for you to harm any of them, seeing as you may have been friends with a few." I stared at him. Did it matter if they were friends or not? They were still living beings, no matter what they were to me.

"I..." I managed, but it came out as a squeak. *Don't be like that*, I chided myself, *these people think they need me, they think I'm strong*. I was going to act like it. I shouldn't act like this. Not in front of anybody, or they might take it all back and just kill me themselves. I shivered, and felt fear creep into me. I pushed it down and put on a confident face. "I'd be happy to become more educated about the Slayers." I smiled, though it was fake. The man looked relieved that I'd agreed. He probably had orders from Vayne to educate me and just wanted cooperation.

"Great," he said. "You can call me Keon. Anyway, I know this might seem weird for you, but I think you should listen to the storyteller tell the kids stories of the Ravens and Slayers. They're all true, and it helps clarify a lot. I'll be there too;

also a lot of other Slayers like to listen. You won't be the only person of your age there."

I frowned; I wasn't too excited about listening to stories. "When and where?" I asked, although I didn't want to go. I didn't miss the stares and occasional glares of people walking by me, and though I made no indication I cared or even noticed, it hit me hard to be disliked. If listening to some stories with this guy would help, I'd do it.

"In the library, right now. You can bring Markus, if you want."

I didn't mind Keon right now, but he seemed like the kind of guy who might get annoying after a while.

Brightening up with the idea of seeing the library, I followed Keon. The idea of inviting Markus entered my mind, but I dismissed it, not really in the mood to hang out with Markus. He was always so cheerful, but I wasn't in the mood for his happiness at the moment.

We went up so many floors, I started to wonder where we were and what type of building we were in. After what felt like a long time going up the elevator, the sliding doors opened into what I could only describe as pure beauty. The wide expanse of the library took up the entire floor, large bookshelves towering so high I couldn't believe anyone could ever pick out a book from the top.

Eight Pillars descended from the roof, circling a point in the middle of the huge dome of glass that was the roof. Vines worked around the out-side of the glass, crawling across it like spiders. The pillars had intricate designs flowing in them and around them, looking handmade. Were they connected to the glass the vines splayed on?

I was overwhelmed by loveliness. At the end of each bookshelf sat a unique statue most likely carved by hand out of wood, and the fierce beasts seemed alive. The middle statue looked similar to a god or goddess, and was stunning.

The floor was covered by mats and rugs, swirling with designs and pictures, matching per-fectly with everything else. Books overflowed the aisles of bookshelves; they seemed tightly packed together to preserve space. The books seemed to range from so old, they were being held together only by a couple strings, to newly published that gleamed in the fierce sunlight already cook-ing me. Keon seemed amused by my reaction to the library, and although I hadn't seen all the rooms in the Slayers' compound, I knew this was my favorite.

"Okay, I know this is really impressive, but please, pick up your jaw. I think you dropped it somewhere," Keon said. I snapped my mouth closed and blushed. "C'mon, they probably already started. This way," he said, disappearing into an aisle. I followed promptly, worried I might get lost if I didn't stay close.

We came to a clearing in the bookshelves, and I guessed this was Storytelling 101. A round mat with bean bag chairs and pillows filled by children of all ages from five to young teens crowded most of the space. But on the opposite side of the mat was a rocking chair where a man sat, surrounded by props I guessed were for the stories. He seemed ancient, with wrinkles surrounding his mouth and nose. A few adults sat in chairs, most leaning forward on the edge to make sure they didn't miss a single word.

"they had to dispose of these, what they called, creatures, because they were strange and uncontrollable, so they went after them. They said terrible things about them, like they were cursed by the devil or deserved worse punishments than death for simply existing."

"Really, they were wrong; they were blessed by an angel that controls all that happens to people after death. The angel prized her creations, and every one who died, she sent back to earth in a safe place. Soon they had a small village, all of them the same. The people who were sent into the village from the angel, they say, emerged from the forest completely naked and shocked and scared."

"Nobody remembered how they got there, but they never forgot the beautiful face that everyone assumed was the angel." He took a breath, and I found a chair near the back. "There were barely one hundred years of creating this village before different people started emerging from the trees."

"These were not like the original people. No,

they had very different powers. The village feared them, but remembered how it felt to be the one emerging from those trees and exiled from the other people, so they let them stay with open arms, trying their best to help them take control of their power."

"For eons, we maintained the sharing of our space with the other people, until we started to slowly drift apart. We stopped working together. They took up one side of the village and we took the other, not ever really mixing. The leaders of the village knew it was only a matter of time until we never talked to each other whatsoever."

"They tried to keep us together, desperately having council meetings to make us as close to each other as we once were. While their efforts bought us a few more years of peace, the truth didn't change. In one of the feasts the council used in an effort to keep us in closer alliance, the people with different powers suddenly, violently attacked us. They penetrated over half our population, and we were forced to leave our village to get away."

"We went three days' journey, and set up camp where we began a new village. Slowly, humans moved in around us, but we kept our identity a secret in case we were still *kill on sight*. Those people who took our land called themselves Ravens, and we, the innocent people who fled, call ourselves Slayers.

"The Ravens stole our land, feigning they were our allies, but really waiting for more of their kind to come from the woods. We tried to help them. We tried so hard, after all those years of working to create that town. We rightfully owned the land, as we arrived three-hundred years before them, building it up until they came and ruined it."

"And that place, our birthplace, is right here in Los Angeles, but also right here in the village we used to call Lost Angels," he finished.

I never realized the Slayer past was so interesting, and since that story was kind of short, I assumed the kids would stay intent on it, as I was still completely engaged. I did dislike how he said the Ravens were. I stopped myself from thinking something nice about the Ravens. They purposely hurt me, made me bend to their every command, and I hated them just like the other Slayers did.

Funny I thought, how the Ravens said the Slayers were so bad and terrible, and yet while I was here they were completely nice, even accepting of me when I came from the Ravens. I still couldn't believe Toby was the leader of the Ravens, but I did think I was over my burst of anger towards him. They did say Toby didn't have anything to do with his rise to power, but for me, that was hard to believe.

Either way, it didn't change the fact that Toby didn't try to stop them from torturing me. Not to mention the way Sarah and Dr. Dobson treated Markus... No, I wasn't going to think about that either. It would only make me mad. Keon leaned toward me.

"This story he's about to tell has no evidence, so it might just be a myth. We don't know. The character is one hundred percent made up, but the other things have a possibility of being true."

"We're not sure this one is true," the man said, backing what Keon spoke of. He put a hand near his lips, acting like he was telling a secret and trying to keep it quiet. "But it's definitely possible," he whispered loudly to the children, and then leaned back in his seat.

"Only one hundred years ago, when it was still common for people to use horses and carriages to get around, someone named Sam was born into the world as a Slayer. He grew up here, serving us proudly, going on mission after mission to help. When he was about twenty years old, he was honored by being sent on an assassination mission to kill the Ravens' leader." He leaned forward again and pretended to whisper to the children. "This person would be Toby's great, great, great-grandfather."

"This was both an honor and a curse, as this mission could very well end his life. Sam went after him; they say he was the stealthiest person one would meet. When he practiced, people gathered around to watch him appear then disappear into shadows.

"Most people thought he would fail this mission. The planning was terrible and the timing wasn't great, but Sam was determined. He managed, and though he came out a month later with a missing arm and gash across his side, he was very alive.

"The uproar he caused in the Ravens' compound was outrageous, and it took all of a year for the descendant - Toby's great, great grandfather - to take control of everyone. The Slayers were proud of Sam, and it became history. After a day of rest, he produced a dagger to show everyone - the dagger of Toby's bloodline, stolen by Sam and brought to us. Everyone was stunned that Sam managed it."

The man leaned down to open a purse looking thing. He gently pulled something out, using both hands to ensure he wouldn't drop it, but being sure to be extra gentle. The dagger case was breathtaking, but the glass was so thick and worn with age I could hardly see the dagger inside. He held it up, and then put it on the floor where children peered at it curiously. "All right, that was all completely true, even with evidence, but this point is where we're not so sure anymore.

"Sam decided, after losing an arm to the assassination, he was going to retire. He stayed in Slayers Tower, living there and teaching kids like you about his journey, displaying that very dagger I showed you. When he was thirty-six years old, he told everyone he was going on a trip for a vacation holiday. Now, Slayers don't usually have vacation holidays, but it seemed nobody cared, saying things like he deserved a vacation, and they all sent him money to fund his trip. They said it was their gift for helping the Slayers.

"He bought a carriage, two horses, and supplies for the journey. Sam's best friend, who also went on the assassination mission, accompanied him on the vacation, and they took turns driving the carriage to the far east coast.

"They stopped at night to let the horses rest and drink in nearby streams and enjoyed themselves away from home. When they reached the ocean, they gave their horses and carriage to a farmer who would take care of them for a small fee until they returned, then paid to go on a boat crossing the ocean.

"After four weeks' time, they reached their destination, a beautiful town in France. They had the foresight to learn French, so they had no problems when they toured, until they found another person like us, but yet, not. Their powers were in the mind. They could influence someone to do something and read their mind. They could make people see things that weren't there and even alter people's thoughts without them noticing.

"Sam and his friend made friends with a couple of them. He learned a great deal. Of course, he was alarmed there were other people like the Ravens and Slayers out there we didn't know about. Friend or foe, he asked himself constantly, when the friends weren't around to read his mind.

"He went as fast as he could back to the Slayers Tower, but it still took him many weeks. Once he got back though, he told everyone about this discovery. Nobody really believed him, but they didn't let it cloud their judgment of the amazing man who killed a Raven leader.

"Of course, the leader of Slayers was very interested. He funded trips for thirty investigators to go to France and find these people, making sure they were indeed friends and to find out if there were others like us. He was quite scared of them and for good reasons, too.

"By reading Sam's mind, they found out everything he knew, including the exact location of the Slayers' Tower. In the end, nobody has ever seen them again. The investigators came back happy from the trip, but disappointed they didn't find any of the mind readers.

"Since then, there have been over two hundred trips to different places around the world looking for others like us, all of which were unsuccessful. Sam had a beautiful family, and died of old age when he was eighty-three years old. " He smiled, and stood. "I'm tired and hungry, aren't you? I think we can continue this tomorrow." He collected his things. "Tomorrow, I will tell you about the disease that plagued us long ago." The kids hopped up, running around the bookshelves, squealing about where they would hide. I stood, and Keon came over.

"That was shorter than I expected," I said.

"Yes, well, Edwin gets so tired so fast these days, he's growing older. The children wouldn't listen much longer without fidgeting anyway, so I guess it's all right."

"Aren't those stories a bit violent for kids? You'd think they'd get nightmares or something."

"We teach them young that harming Ravens is all right, and that violence is nothing to be afraid of. Our kind is meant to know what it means to fight."

"Oh," I replied, half-stunned, half-horrified.

"Well, I hope that changed your view of the Ravens, even in the slightest. But, it seems to be getting close to dinnertime. You wouldn't want to be late," Keon said, and I smiled.

"No, I wouldn't want to be late. Thank you."

Keon looked over his shoulder. "I suppose this is your first time in the library. Follow me; I'll lead you to the exit." As we walked, he added, "Most people get lost on their first trip."

"I can see why," I grumbled as we reached the door. Keon stopped.

"Well, I have a meeting with Mr. Zahavi in twenty minutes here; maybe tomorrow we'll do something like this again."

"Okay. After my training I could."

"I know. In fact, I think tomorrow is church day, actually."

Church day? Sunday? I was kind of confused, but I was hungry so I thanked Keon, before making my way to the kitchen. I could tell tomorrow was going to be so fun. I hovered in the halls, taking my time to reach the dining area. I still had ten minutes.

A couple minutes later, I arrived at the kitchen, and of course, David and Markus were already at a table trying to wave me over. I weaved through the small crowd and sat. Markus pushed me a plate of mashed potatoes and a bowl of soup.

"What have you been up to?" David asked between bites.

"I was listening to some of the history of the Slayers. It's pretty interesting," I said, and then took a spoonful of soup. He stared at me for a moment.

"You think that is interesting?" He was almost gawking.

"Well, it's kinda cool."

"*Cool?* When I was a kid, I had to study that stuff, and my god to hell, it was definitely *not* interesting *or* cool."

"Studying it is different. I was just listening to the stories."

"Same thing," David grumbled, and shoveled another bucket load of soup into his mouth. I focused on eating, taking small bites.

"Marry, I think Vayne is trying to wave to you, you better at least look up," Markus said, smiling as if it was hilarious. I looked up, and sure enough, Vayne was politely nodding to everyone, wearing a white suit with a black tie to match his hair. When he saw me look up, he waved, coming my way. I silently prayed he wouldn't eat dinner with us. Once he was in hearing distance, I could see he was beaming as if he were the sun.

"Hi, Vayne," I said. He smiled.

"Hello."

"Did you need something?" I asked.

"I've decided the time you will meet the Slayers. Tomorrow at church would just be so much better for everyone, and I think you probably are settled in by now. I sent Keon to help you, how did that go?" he asked politely.

"It was great. So...I'm going to meet the Slayers tomorrow?" I asked. No. I couldn't. I didn't know what to wear. What to say. What would I do?

"Yes, everyone is really eager to meet you and know your story like I do, and although I'd be delighted to tell the story, I think it'd be *so* much better if you told it," he said.

I silently groaned. I didn't want to, not at all. I was about to ask what to wear, but then remembered Markus and David would not turn up a chance to tease me twenty-four-seven if they heard me asking something like that. What if they wanted a display of my power? What if I couldn't do it in front of all those people? I was panicking, but I hoped to hell my face didn't look like it.

"All right, great," I said pleasantly, as if I wasn't freaking out.

"I'll send someone to get you ready. It'll be pretty early in the morning, so remember to wake her up, Markus." He addressed my friend at the end. I had no doubt he would remember. Vayne looked at his watch.

"Hmm. Well, I have to go now. I have a meeting. I'll see you tomorrow then, Marry. Take care." He slowly turned and weaved into the crowd. Markus took two more bites, and then jumped up.

"We're going to practice. Right now," he said, already pulling me towards the hallway. I followed willingly, although I was confused.

"Why?" I asked.

"Because. You know why. They're going to want you to demonstrate your powers, but I thought we'd have more time than this," Markus said, still pulling me down the hall. We were already half way there.

"We will work all night if that's what it takes to let you use at least an electricity bolt," he said. I glanced over my shoulder, and as predicted, David was following a short distance down the hall. Markus pulled me into the training room a little too hard when I was looking over my shoulder, and I stumbled and would have fallen if he hadn't caught me.

"Thanks," I said. His hands were still on my arms, making sure I was stable. He nodded, and then let his hands back down to his sides. He looked at a padded wall on the other side of the training room and pointed to it.

"Hit it from here," he said.

"What?"

"Do it." David interrupted, walking into the

training room. "You really need to be able to use it. If you can't, the Slayers will think you're just a pest Vayne is obsessed with."

"I don't think I can."

"I know you can," Markus said, and then shaped his hands into a sphere and bowed. "Do the magic, wise one," he said, smiling. "Focus."

"Funny." I closed my eyes, and imagined a blue electric shock so thick and powerful it could dent the wall. I imagined it cracking with such force of electricity it could power the whole building, imagined it flying out of my core and pushing against it. Nothing happened, but I kept envisioning the green electric shock forcing itself out of me. I thought of it as a balloon being squished - the air needing to escape. Two hands locked around my wrists.

"Marry - stop!" Markus shouted, but then his hands suddenly disappeared from my wrists, and my eyes flew open. As soon as my focus dropped the green electric beam shattered, and I saw the wall across from us had been completely destroyed and mangled. I could see the other room through the wall, but that wasn't what frightened me.

Markus cowered at a far wall, cradling his hands. David focused hard on me, as if there was a threat. His position looked far too aggressive to be aimed at me, so I spun around to see what was happening, my face draining of color. Were Ravens attacking, right now? When I saw there were no intruders, I turned back and took a step towards Markus, intending to make sure everything was okay.

He cowered farther from me, and I was sure I would have preferred a stab to the chest than the pain the motion caused me. But then I realized.

I was the intruder, I was the threat. I was the one who hurt Markus. David put his hand out.

"Marry, are you sure you're done? Do you have complete control?" he asked. "Markus got shocked when he touched you. Your body was engulfed with electricity." Panicking, the realization set in that *I* hurt Markus. I needed to make sure he was okay, I wouldn't just leave him. We needed to take him to the medical room.

"I have control," I said, taking an experimental step towards Markus. He seemed to release a breath. He didn't cower when I approached him.

"What did I do to you? Show me your hands." When he hesitated, I touched his arm. "I'm sorry. I'm so, so sorry, Markus. I shouldn't have lost control like that. I need to take you to the medic. You need to be healed." Honestly? I wasn't in the least worried about the wall. David drifted to the corner of the room, and it seemed like he wanted to get out. "What?" I said as I looked at Markus's exposed hands. Holding his hands gently in mine, I examined the black splotches on each that I knew were hurting him.

"Marry, you were amazing," he said. How could

he say that? I hurt him. His pain was all my fault, and he was calling me *amazing*. Who did that?

"I... I did this to you," I said. "Oh, Markus, I'm so sorry. I should have been more careful." The black splotches were bleeding slowly, and they looked horrible. Markus just stared at me.

"It was amazing. I haven't seen another Slayer ever do anything with that amount of power. It was pure power, no light or trickery involved," Markus said. I couldn't help feeling a little proud, but when I looked back at Markus's hands again, I was horrified with myself.

"I'm a horrible person..." I whispered, looking at Markus's burns. He pulled out of my grip and rested a few of his fingers on my cheek, ever so lightly.

"You're not horrible. It was an accident. I'll be fine, anyway," he said and let his hand drop.

"I know but... I still did it. It's still my fault." I let go of Markus's other hand, and he let it fall to his side. "Let's just... go to the infirmary. I need you to be healed," I said. Markus grumbled, and stalked toward the door. I followed him, listening to his grumbles and hating myself for hurting him.

Once we made it to the infirmary, a Follower was more than happy to heal Markus up while drilling me like I was some sort of celebrity. She asked things like how powerful I was and if I could really use both Slayer and Raven power, which I could. Markus didn't blame me even once for hurting him, but I still felt bad. I couldn't believe he'd forgive me so easily. It was me who hurt him, but I really didn't mean to. Markus understood that. I was so thankful for him, he never stopped helping me.

CHAPTER TWENTY

MARRY

"This one is just *beautiful*, dear. What do you think?" Lynn asked, holding up a dress from the armoire. Lynn was the helper lady sent by Vayne to help me dress. She'd been trying to find me an outfit for what seemed like *forever*, even though it had only been fifteen minutes of me turning down dresses because the fabric felt weird. I shook my head.

"That one looks too puffy. I'd be swimming in fabric."

Lynn shoved it back into the armoire and grabbed another dress, yanking it out. It had two layers of fabric, the first was a solid white and the next a see-through layer of black, tinting the white, making it look gray and full-black in some places depending on how you looked at it. There was a white band just above where my elbows would be, and on the side was a design that looked sort of like a gray flower with coiled white vines going down to the waist.

"There is *no* reason you wouldn't like this one. It's beautiful, it's not too puffy, and it's soft and stretchy. Go try it on and if it fits we will do your hair," Lynn said as she thrust the dress into my hands. The inside that was supposed to be soft felt more like rough, but in my fifteen minutes with Lynn, I've never met someone so stubborn. Vayne probably sent her to me on purpose.

"Go ahead! I can't wait to see it on you," Lynn chirped. "I'll be waiting, right here."

I changed into the dress, and as I expected, it wasn't comfortable in the least. It really did look beautiful though. The fabric went to the floor, but surprisingly didn't drag; I didn't feel like I'd trip on it. I went back to the main room where Lynn was waiting, and when I opened the door she was automatically hovering over me, looking at the dress from all angles, adjusting random things that didn't matter, and doing whatever else she did. Finally she backed away and looked at it.

"Dear, you will be the most beautiful girl in this whole building after I do your hair. Markus will be *so* impressed with how you look," Lynn said, winking. I opened my mouth to comment

198

on the Markus part, but Lynn was already speaking. "Let's get your hair done, and quickly. We wouldn't want to keep Vayne waiting!" Lynn said, dragging me into the bathroom with a chair in her other hand. She was strong; I had to give her that. She plunked the chair in front of the mirror and motioned for me to sit. After I sat, she brushed my tangled hair, carefully straightening the knots and letting it lay flat on by back and shoulders.

"Straighten or curl it, do you think?" Lynn asked me, looking at my bangs in the mirror.

"I think it looks fine as it is," I said mostly because I was hungry and wanted to eat. She ignored my comment.

"Oh, I have the greatest idea." She reached around me to open a drawer I hadn't noticed until then. She riffled through it, and then pulled out a plastic bag of small black jewels that were probably fake. She smiled proudly, opening the bag and putting the small diamonds in my long waves.

A couple minutes later, she finished, but it felt more like hours. I looked at her work in the mirror, and was stunned when I saw the former knots fall over my shoulders in contained waves with small black jewels littering the locks of hair. I smiled, happy with the look, even though the jewels made it feel like I was carrying boulders on my head.

"You like it?" Lynn asked after a second, and I stood, twisting so I could see the back.

"I love it. Looks great. Thank you." She waved off the thank you.

"Okay, I'm done. You look fabulous, but you're probably starved by now, you poor thing. You stay here and I'll fetch Markus to tell him you're ready," she said, hurrying out the door. I went out to the main area and looked through the shoes. Lynn was probably going to make me wear specific ones, but I didn't really have anything else to do.

A couple minutes later, Lynn came in happily with Markus, who was bickering with Lynn about how his clothing was fine. When Lynn got inside the room she hurried over to me, frantically looking through the shoes.

"Oh heavens, I forgot about shoes! My dear, you should have reminded me!" she muttered, pulling out a pair of shoes that looked like they matched my dress, which was *very* itchy and uncomfortable.

"Here we are; these will have to do." She tossed me shoes. "Try them on." I glanced at Markus, and he looked like he was going to laugh. He was wearing formal-looking jeans and a white T-shirt with a black coat over top, and he looked handsome in it. I hated that I even noticed that. I glared at him, pulling on a shoe. It felt like my foot was being resized. At every angle, the shoe squeezed, and my toes were like potatoes, mashed together at the end. Lynn looked at the shoes.

"Great. They are *wonderful*," she exclaimed, hurrying back to Markus.

"These are a bit small."

"Shh, they look nice. That's all that matters, yes?" she said, not even glancing at me as she fussed over Markus.

"Well - yes, but these are like *really* small."

"No, no, no, they are fine. You're keeping those shoes on. They look absolutely *adorable*," she said. "Now, Markus, why isn't this shirt tucked in? Also, tighten up your belt, it's practically *sagging...*" I stopped listening to her one-sided conversation, standing in the tiny shoes. These were made for my toes to fit in, not my whole feet.

"So, Lynn, I think me and Markus have to go. If Vayne wanted Markus to have breakfast with him, he might be late. We wouldn't want to be late for Vayne, would we?" I said, interrupting whatever she was saying and walking to the door.

"Yeah, um, I think we have to go. And as much as I appreciate you trying to help me look nice, you're gonna have to stop so I can leave," Markus said. I grinned at nothing in particular.

"What?" Markus asked me when he came to the door.

"Nothing," I replied. "It's just funny she was fussing over you."

"Oh, so now she's only allowed to fuss over you?" Markus said. I rolled my eyes and motioned for Markus to lead the way to Vayne's room. He strode out, and I followed right behind him.

We arrived at Vayne's door, and before we even knocked the door flung open to Vayne smiling cheerfully.

"There you are, my magician. The Slayers cannot *wait* to meet you." He stepped back. "Come in, eat something. You must be starving," Vayne said. I walked in and sat on the couch where I sat last time. Markus sat beside me.

The room was quite large, but the corner we occupied was more crowded with furniture than spacious. There were beads hanging from the ceiling acting as a room divider, and behind them I could make out a bed and small table. There was a coffee table in between the two couches filled with food, and I basically drooled.

"Marry, I really must say Lynn did a magnificent job dressing you. You look wonderful," Vayne said.

"Thank you. Lynn was really great; she helped me pick this dress and helped with my hair," I said, reaching over and pulling a plate of cut apples out of the pile and munching on them. Markus grabbed three granola bars - the most unhealthy thing there - and opened one of them.

"So, Vayne, what am I going to be doing, exactly? Just meeting them and saying hi?" I asked. I knew the hope was naïve, but I kind of wished I would only be saying hi.

"The Slayers are most interested in your powers. They are wishing with all their hearts they will see some electricity around you, and they want you to explain your story to them. It's up to you, of course, but I know the depth of their wishes. They want to understand you better."

I gulped down a piece of apple. I didn't really know how to control any sort of electricity without it connecting to my body, and even with it connecting, I still didn't know how to use it. I would probably do too much power or too little. And in front of all those people... They could get hurt like Markus did. I forced myself to smile.

"Great," I said in what I wanted to be an excited voice. I munched one more bite of apple, and then sat back. Markus put his granola bar wrappers on the table.

"You understand that the Slayers are convinced you are a message sent from the gods, a goddess yourself even, correct?" Vayne asked, as if I was a student and he, a teacher.

"Right. Almost forgot about that bit," I said, hoping I didn't sound *too* annoyed.

"Also, my family isn't feeling so well this morning, so we won't be meeting them today," Vayne said.

"Of course. I hope they feel better soon," I replied.

"I'll tell them," Vayne sighed.

"When can we go?" I asked. Vayne practically jumped out of his seat.

"If you're ready now, shall we?"

I stood and followed him and Markus into the hall. Vayne seemed to almost run through the hallways as we followed him to the church. Markus and I had to jog to keep up.

"Church will be starting in another twenty minutes, but you and I are required to be there plenty early. I'm also very sorry, but Markus you will have to wait outside or find something else to do until it's time for church. Only Marry and I will be in front of the people, along with the priest," Vayne said.

I took a deep nervous breath. I was mostly banking on luck if they asked me to use my powers, because I wasn't really in control of it yet. Following Vayne was like trying to outrun an athlete - almost impossible. Several times already I had to guess which hallway he turned down. Markus eventually drifted off somewhere without us, probably getting a chocolate bar or bottle of soda from somewhere.

Vayne stopped at a set of huge double doors, and knocked twice. The doors rattled open, and a little servant girl stood in our path. Vayne strode past her and into the giant room. I followed, my mouth dropping open at the rows and rows of empty seating, each bench filled with intricate designs that looked carved by hand. There were easily fifty benches on each side.

In the front, there was a big balcony set quite high off the ground. Two twirling sets of mahogany staircases led to it. Vayne walked a path in the middle of all the benches, and he seemed to be leading to the balcony. Not much of a surprise there, he did say he, I and the priest were to be up in front.

After a hike past all the benches, we finally climbed the staircase to the balcony. I followed Vayne all the way up, then gawked at where we came in. No wonder the room was so bright. The entire back wall was stained glass. The designs of different gods and devils and angels were amazing.

"It's not too stylish when you see it from the outside," Vayne admitted. "But I think the inside view really is worth it."

"So what do we do now? Just wait?" I asked.

"Yes. We will wait for the priest to come, and when he arrives, he will let in the crowd from outside. It will take the people around five minutes to take their seats, but when they do, the priest will start."

"Okay," I said. The wait for the doors to open didn't feel as long as I expected. Probably because I was too busy sweating in fear of the people who wanted me to show off my powers. I inhaled, trying to calm myself. It worked, somewhat. I wished my family was here to comfort me. Grant and Dad would know just what to do to make me feel better, even if they didn't know they were helping. I wondered where this Slayer's place was and how Grand and my Dad were feeling right now. Hopefully they were doing alright. Maybe Toby never stopped curing them. If they've been getting better all this time, they're probably on their feet by now.

Hearing a steady knocking at the back of the room, I whipped my head up, turning my gaze to the door. It drummed steadily for ten beats and then a bell rang, and the doors opened to a giant crowd of people.

Hundreds of people flooded into the church. As I watched, I noted there weren't many seniors, and the ones that were there looked extremely old. I noticed all the people remained silent, only speaking when it was important or to answer a young child's question.

There were so many people already taking up half of the church and more still poured in. I didn't know there were that many rooms in the building for all these people. There were easily two hundred and counting.

The priest arrived beside Vayne on the balcony we were standing on, and he told Vayne something I couldn't hear. He nodded and turned to me.

"Time for us to sit," he said and walked to the side where a few fold-out chairs were propped against the wall. I grabbed one and unfolded it, sitting next to Vayne. I heard only slight chatter below, but other than that, the crowd was quiet, apart from the fairly loud clunk of shoes as they walked to find a spot to sit. The priest turned from the audience and Vayne took a small square from his jacket and handed it to the priest, who then faced the audience again.

After a couple minutes, everyone was finally seated. The priest held the square Vayne gave him up to his mouth, and cleared his throat. The noise was projected throughout the room by speakers. Everyone fell silent instantly.

"Hello, everyone. Thank you for coming to our weekly church ceremony today," the priest said. "I'd like to say our thank-yous to the god that blessed us with this extraordinary power of electricity, for protecting us when we needed it, for giving us a defense against the Ravens, and for letting us protect the humans and ourselves. The best way for us to communicate our gratitude strong enough is through song, so we shall sing. Thank you again, almighty god, for blessing us with these extraordinary gifts." Everyone stood, including Vayne, so I followed his lead.

"We shall all tell you how thankful we are," the priest said, and everyone sang. It wasn't in words, at least not in this language, but it sounded soothing and calm and happy and everything anyone would ever want for a lullaby. Vayne didn't sing, so I didn't either. The voices of so many people together was very loud, but completely in tune.

It was beautiful, much better than any other music I had ever heard. The song was compassionate and intense and unforgiving at the same time, going harmoniously with the tune and all the voices. The church service went on, going through protocol mostly, we said prayers about winning against the Ravens in a big war, prayers for Vayne, and we had some holy water thrown around.

"Now, as you all know, we have a special guest today," the priest said. "Marry, would you stand?" I stood, and took a step forward. I smiled at the people. There were so many of them. Hundreds and hundreds I would disappoint and embarrass myself in front of if I screwed this up. I twiddled my thumbs behind my back.

"So, Marry, we've all been terribly curious; how did you wind up here?" he asked. He offered me the small square, and I held it to my mouth as he had.

"That would be a long story," I said. "At first, I was at school, a normal student, and the Ravens sort of captured me, I guess. They blackmailed me into joining their side, or they would kill my family. At least, the family I have left." I took a deep breath. "Later on, I got angry that someone was hurting and abusing some of my... friends, so I hurt the man who was doing it.

"As a result, they put me in a jail sort of place. I stayed there for a while, and then they decided to do experiments on me. Another of my friends, who was with them at the time, stood up for me when one of the experiments especially hurt, and he got punished as well. I was so angry, and I had to protect him, and ended back in the jail again. I decided I didn't want to put up with it anymore, so I left." The priest took the square from me.

"How did you get away?" he asked, and then

handed the mic back to me. This was going all right so far, I was almost done.

"I escaped, but I'm not going into details. One of the people I worked with helped me get out. Once I was out, there were several Ravens sent to bring me back. They attacked us, and I somehow knocked them all out, but I also fainted. My two friends who were helping me escape said they didn't know where to go, so they brought me to you." I finished, handing the square back to the priest.

"I really hate to ask this, but could you show us a demonstration of your powers? I know all of us are just itching to see," he said, turning to the audience who all nodded in agreement. My breathing hitched, but I smiled. Sweat pooled on my brows, and I closed my eyes so I could concentrate on summoning the power. I stood there for almost half a minute, trying my hardest to summon it - anything. If only I could just summon that beam of light, but have it only light and not strength.

I heard a window smash, shattering my concentration, and my eyes flew open to chaos. Ravens poured through the windows, doors, everywhere. They slaughtered the surprised Slayers without mercy, and by the time the few guards that were armed were fighting, at least fifty were already dead or wounded.

I gripped the railing of the balcony, tears falling, searching anxiously for Markus in the crowd.

I saw groups of four to five Followers holding hands concentrating, and realized they were trying to suppress the sounds and sights of this massacre from the humans outside the building.

The Slayers were extremely organized, sending out groups of twenty to get weapons for the rest of them. All the Slayers had right then was their magic, and they were using it to their full extent. The guards defended them as best they could with their weapons, trying to stop the Ravens from getting too close to the Slayers. There were also animals shredding through the Slayers, and I realized it was the Ravens shape shifting.

In one of the groups of Followers, I was horrified to see Kayla in a circle of five. She was so young. She shouldn't be a part of this.

I gasped in horror when I saw Markus in the crowd. He was lying perfectly still in the middle of four other followers, claw-like gashes running through his chest. I guessed he was probably a part of that group covering the sounds until he got injured. Of course, that's all it was. He was only injured.

Looking around frantically, I felt more hot tears drop down my face as more people died. I whipped around and took the stairs to the floor two at a time. There were so many people, I didn't know if I could get to Markus in time. He was bleeding badly, and I didn't know if he would make it much longer unless someone stopped the outflow of blood.

It was impossible to do anything in the chaos around me, and this dress was interfering with my running. Stumbling around in this crowd was like trying to navigate a maze, and trying to find Markus, some sort of side quest. I didn't even know why anyone wasn't trying to kill me, but they hadn't tried yet, and I didn't care if they did. All I cared about was finding Markus and then stopping this battle. I saw a group of Followers, and I yanked one from the circle. The remaining three Followers didn't falter; they just filled the gap.

"Please - please, follow me; I need you to heal someone," I gasped out. The Follower was yanking on my grip, but I barely felt it.

"No, I can't; I need to help them, they can barely stop the sounds from escaping to the humans!"

"I need you to help me, please! It will just be a second - he'll die without you!" I snapped at her. Pulling her deeper into the crowds, I tried desperately to find Markus. People started noticing me and the Follower, and before I could even react, someone was pulling back a spear to stab me, but he collapsed before he could manage it. I didn't see what happened but it saved my life. I kept working through the crowd.

In a break of the chaos, I thought I saw Markus. Shoving people out of the way, I ducked under the hands of the Followers around Markus. When I reached him I fell to the ground and looked at the wound. I turned to the Follower I'd brought with me.

"Please! Help him! Don't just stand there! Heal the wounds!" I exclaimed. He was dying. There was too much blood, the wound was too deep. She had to heal it now or he'd die. "NOW!" I screamed. The Follower kneeled next to him, checking his pulse.

"I can't heal him - he'll need like three..."

"Try! Do anything you need to! Just heal him! PLEASE!" I sobbed. The Follower leaned back.

"I can't. There's nothing I can do. He'll be dead in a minute, and I can't bring him back," she said, and disappeared in the crowd. I sobbed over Markus, avoiding looking at the wound. Flashes of light blurred the edges of my vision, but I didn't know if they were my electricity or someone else's. The only person who ever cared about me even in the slightest was about to die, and I was watching it happen.

Tendrils of wispy air was coming out of my fingertips, circling Markus's body, but I could have been imagining it. The blue tendrils now looked like threads, floating through the air. They were beautiful. The wisps focused on the wound, but I refused to stop looking at his face. His bloodied face that was still the same as when I first met him. He stopped breathing, and there was definitely too much blood on the floor for him to remain alive, and when I took his pulse, another sob burst out of me. He was dead. He was officially dead.

But then he gasped in a breath.

And then the blood retreated back into him flowing like a creek in reverse, and color returned to his face.

My world came back together, by this amazing miracle that brought Markus to life, that funny person who was one of my few friends. He seemed completely unaware of why I was crying, and he sat up easily. When he saw his surroundings, he instantly remembered or at least understood, I didn't even know. He turned to me quickly.

"You need to get out of here – Now! I have to help the Followers, they really need help. They can barely stop the sound. They're sending us messages in our minds."

"Markus?" I said in awe. He came Back To Life!

"I'm right here, look, we can talk about it later, whatever it is, but you have to leave."

"You were... You were dead."

"Oh, my god Marry, just get out of here!" he yelled. I knew he was right - I should leave or do something. I hoped he would be okay, and he looked fine. I nodded.

"Okay - okay. Take care of yourself, don't get hurt. I'll kill you if you die." Markus laughed unsteadily, and stood.

"Get yourself to safety, Marry." I got up too, ducking under the hands of the Followers as I tried to work my way through the bloodbath. Bodies were littered everywhere, both Slayer and Raven alike, and the smell of blood was thick in the air. There was so much death that I could barely see through the crowd enough to sort of understand what was happening. I could see the group of Slayers surrounding Vayne in order to protect him, and I could see Toby behind all the Ravens ordering people to do this or that. So many people had died at the hands of the Ravens and the Slayers, I couldn't bear it.

I saw the door, but it was blocked by Ravens. Just then I realized how tired I was, and I assumed it was from the magic I used to defend myself. It wore me out, though I didn't really think I used it that much.

A huge snake slithered under Vayne's guards and tripped almost half of them, then went for their necks. I knew instantly it was a shape shifter, and it was going to kill all of those people if I didn't do something. I tried to summon my power, but it wouldn't come. I tried to *force* it to come, but it was no use.

Grabbing a broken metal bar off the ground, I went towards the snake. I didn't know if I could actually kill it, since it wasn't human, but I could at least try to disable it so it wouldn't hurt anyone else. I cursed a string of very vulgar swears when my dress started snagging on my feet and tripping me, and while I inwardly cringed at my language, I marched on toward the snake.

I was just about there when a Raven tackled me to the ground and threw the metal bar from my grasp. I thrashed under him, trying to get free, but he wouldn't budge. After a few seconds of thrashing, I realized he didn't intend to kill me and released a breath - at least I wouldn't die yet. Out of the corner of my eye I saw more people die at the hands of Slayers, and I shrunk back from the chaos as far as I could, being that I was pinned to the ground.

"Please," I gasped. "make them stop. Make everyone stop killing!"

"We're only making the world a better place," he spat.

"I don't know why Blake wants you so badly. You can't even stand to hurt people who have killed thousands," he said, reaching into his back pocket and taking out a dagger, pushing it against my throat. Maybe he really was going to kill me. Maybe he didn't care if he wasn't supposed to. A small sob escaped me, and he pushed the dagger harder against my skin.

"Blake won't know it was me, and even if he does, it will be worth the pleasure of killing your pretty little face," he said and pushed the dagger harder into my skin. Feeling a line of hot blood trail down my neck and drip onto the floor, I couldn't help but panic. I didn't know what to do. This guy would kill me, and I couldn't do anything about it.

I thrashed again, and this time he lifted off me, but it wasn't from me. Behind him stood Toby, but he wasn't going for me, he pounded the guy who took me down. I scrambled to get up, never taking my eyes off Toby. I made my way to Vayne, but I could see Toby was following faster than I could lead.

I pushed on, and when I was within yelling distance of them, Toby grabbed my arm and pulled me back. I screamed for a weapon, yelling at Vayne, but I didn't know if it would do much good. A Slayer from Vayne's guard noticed me, and rushed over to help. He shot Toby with an electric beam, and Toby let me go, stalking towards the Slayer.

The Slayer who helped me threw something towards me but I failed to catch it, and the object fell on the floor. I snatched the pistol off the ground, it had a giant silencer.

Someone grabbed my arm from behind and swung me around, holding a knife to my throat. I kneed him in the groin and pointed my gun at his forehead. He froze and dropped his weapons.

"Please. I'm not ready to die yet."

"I'm not gonna kill you, just- just get out."

He nodded and scrambled to get away from me. I turned to Toby; he was obviously winning over the Slayer. He was hardly even harmed and the Slayer seemed to barely be able to move. I held the gun up and aimed it at Toby.

"Toby!" I said, making sure he heard me. He glanced over, freezing in place when he saw the gun. He let go of the metal bar he was carrying - the one I dropped - and took a step backwards.

"You see that?" I asked, pointing to a dead

body with my empty hand. "That wouldn't have happened if you and your stupid little gang hadn't come in here and start slaughtering all of us," I said. "Make them stop fighting, right now." Toby shrugged.

"Can't. The Slayers will just kill us all if we stop."

My hand flicked to the side on its own, and all the noises in the room stopped other than mild breathing. My strength suddenly zapped, but I managed to remain upright. I knew I'd done something, and as I looked around, realized people were mid-movement, frozen in place. All they could do was breathe. I could feel my energy draining fast, and I knew it was because I was using so much magic. I was surprised I didn't just collapse.

"What did you do to us?" a Raven asked, lips stiff.

"You can't move. That's it," I replied, mostly guessing.

"Shoot him, Marry. Do it. You have to," Vayne said. "Remember those stories you heard? That was his grandfather. His blood killing ours."

Toby held his hands up, looking straight at the gun pointed at him. I noted he could move but didn't try to stop it. I was too focused on the fact I was holding a gun to a... teenager = someone my age. My hand quivered on the gun handle, and I gripped it tighter, keeping it pointed at Toby.

Sweat dripped down my brow, and my hand was becoming slippery.

"Please, Marry. Don't do this," Toby said. My arm shook, and I held the gun tighter. I could feel the trigger under my index finger; feel every design on the side of the gun. My eyes squeezed shut.

"Marry, please. You know who I really am. You're one of the only people who has seen me."

I opened my eyes, and a tear leaked onto my cheek. I thought about what I was about to do, and as I looked at this broken boy who was forced to become a leader, the boy who offered to be one of my only friends, the boy who had no choice but to lead this awful life and even protested it, I realized I really didn't have to kill him. Nobody could make me.

It was my choice.

The gun clattered to the floor.

Authors Note

Thank you for reading my debut novel "The Ravens". It matters way more to me than you know. I hope you enjoyed it as much as I enjoyed writing it, because I had so much fun. If you really liked it and want to support me, leaving a review on Amazon or liking me on Facebook are some of the best things you can do to help. However, if you want to leave a review on another website, feel free to! It helps me out a lot.

Again, thank you so much for reading and coming with me on this amazing journey. Publishing this book was so fun for me and I can hardly believe it's actually happened. Shannon Mayer made this all possible for me, without her I'm not sure I would have ever even thought of doing it. Thank you Shannon!

ABOUT THE AUTHOR

Katie Faith is a twelve-year-old author of Fantasy who loves to read and write. She lives on a farm in British Columbia, Canada, but does not want to become a farmer when she grows up, so instead pursued writing. Katie never thought she'd be able to write a whole novel, at least not until she met bestselling author Shannon Mayer who offered to take Katie under her wing.

Katie, when not reading or writing spends her time hanging out with friends, playing pointless videogames on the internet, and drawing/watching Anime shows. All of those activities also help Katie get over writers block.

Go to Katie's Facebook page to hear updates about her writing!

Facebook.com/KatieFaithWrites

katiefaithauthor.com